Hungry Like a Wolf

VIKINGS ROCK!
Book 3

by Lily Harlem

"Sex, Drugs, & Rock 'n' Row

ARE YOU SIGNED UP FOR DRAGONBLADE'S BLOG?

You'll get the latest news and information on exclusive giveaways, exclusive excerpts, coming releases, sales, free books, cover reveals and more.

Check out our complete list of authors, too!

No spam, no junk. That's a promise!

Sign Up Here

www.dragonbladepublishing.com

Dearest Reader;

Thank you for your support of a small press. At Dragonblade Publishing, we strive to bring you the highest quality Historical Romance from some of the best authors in the business. Without your support, there is no 'us', so we sincerely hope you adore these stories and find some new favorite authors along the way.

Happy Reading!

CEO, Dragonblade Publishing

Additional Dragonblade books by
Author Lily Harlem

VIKINGS ROCK!
Bats Out of Hell (Book 1)
Holding On for a Hero (Book 2)
Hungry Like a Wolf (Book 3)

Hawk Castle Series
Loved by the Last Knight (Book 1)
Adored by the Archduke (Book 2)
Embraced by the Emperor (Book 3)

The Lyon's Den Series
Lyon at the Altar

Recap of the story so far...

Thank you for picking up the third book in the VIKINGS ROCK! series. I hope you enjoy Ravn and Carmel's story. If it's been a while since you read BATS OUT OF HELL and HOLDING ON FOR A HERO, here is a quick recap.

In the far north of Norway, a battle for the crown of Drangar split a family in two with siblings Haakon, Astrid, and Orm sailing away for a new life in new lands and leaving their brother, Ravn, with their father. Ravn, with a pregnant wife and infant son, lost most of his family but had secured his precious crown.

The traveling Vikings landed on the shores of Lothlend (now Scotland) and settled into the village of Tillicoulty. Settled? No, they invaded and stayed with Haakon announcing himself as king, a fact that angered King Athol—the mean, old, tax-collecting king who made his way to the village once a year with his army to intimidate and demand.

Haakon claimed pretty and feisty village woman Kenna to be his queen. After a falling-out with her brother, Astrid stomped away from the village to live on her own and await passage north.

However, Hamish, Kenna's brother, followed her, intrigued, curious, and protective of the wild foreign shield maiden. Their turbulent love story saw them come together despite her dislike of all things Christian and her devotion to the runes and her Norse gods.

Book Two ended after a big battle with King Athol to protect the village. There were bloody losses plus a princess thrall taken. This is where we pick up in Tillicoulty, though first we must sail to Drangar and check in on King Ravn. Happy reading.

Chapter One

KING RAVN, SON of Rhalson and ruler of Drangar, slit the throat of a dark-brown rat and laid it on a wooden shelf as an offering to Thor. Ravn's chest was tight and his body as heavy as steel. He knew his heart beat because his pulse thudded in his ears, but why it still did… *how* it still could… he didn't know.

"Almighty one," he said, dropping to his knees and clasping his hands on his thighs, "I give you this offering in the hope of forgiveness." He might have been a king, but right now, it felt as though the gods cared nothing for him. And he knew why.

"I beg for your forgiveness, Thor," he repeated, looking up at the stone statue with the square chin, narrowed eyes, and bulky hammer. "I wanted power so badly that I did not think like a king. I stooped low to take that power, so low, and it has cost me dearly. It has cost me everything."

It was true he still had his infant son, Thormod, and his people still respected him, but Ravn was desolate.

"I have paid the price," he said, his throat constricting as he fought emotion. "You took my father to Valhalla to feast with you not a week after my twin brother, Haakon, left Drangar, taking my sister, Astrid, and brother Orm with him. My father's broken heart was no longer able to beat without them."

He paused, thinking of the moment he'd found his aged father dead in his bed, his mouth open and his wise, old eyes unseeing. He'd been holding a small figure of a horse Astrid had carved for him many years ago. "And my wife…dear, sweet

Siggy, you took her too, along with our unborn child."

He paused, unable to speak, and added several apple offerings, setting them neatly alongside the rat.

"You have punished me enough," he said. "And I have learned my lesson. I promise you and the All Father and all the almighty gods that I will atone for my actions, that I will make good my wrongs." He picked up a goblet of wine and poured a few splashes beside the apples and over the rat. "Please accept these gifts and sacrifice. I beg you to reroute my destiny. To send me on a path of purpose and victory so that for the rest of the moons of my life, I can serve."

He closed his eyes. Outside his grand longhouse in Drangar, the easterly wind buffeted the roof and door. Thormod slept in his cot and his slave and friend Joseph had left some time ago.

He was glad that Thormod had settled. Since losing his mother, he'd been fractious and weepy, asking for her constantly and holding out his arms as if reaching for her. He just didn't understand.

It broke Ravn's heart all the more.

A single tear escaped and he dashed it away. He was a king! He didn't cry. He was a Viking warrior, a wolf of the seas, a raider and ruler. He was made of steel interwoven with passion and intelligence.

Except all of those qualities felt like they belonged to a different man right now. It was as if he'd shrunk inside, shriveled, and he didn't know how to stand tall again.

With a sigh, he walked to the fire trough. He added a few more logs to keep the longhouse warm overnight. Not that he was likely to sleep himself. Sleep was as elusive as a white elk these days.

He poured mead and sat on a chair soft with furs and watched the flames leaping to life, curing around the wood, licking and stroking as though caressing it.

He missed his wife's touch, her scent, her sweet taste.

Would he ever marry another, or was she his destiny? Was

Thormod to be his only son?

A dog barked outside and within a few seconds came the loud rattle of hailstones on the roof and far wall.

Ravn looked over at the image of Thor. He was the ruler of hail. Had he heard Ravn's words? Seen his desperation? Was he replying?

The clatter increased, becoming deafening, and he hoped it wouldn't wake his son.

Astrid's face came to mind, so pretty yet vicious with it. He'd never quite known how to handle his sister the way Haakon had. Never been able to get more than a few minutes of softness from her. But if she were at his side now, she'd remind him of the ninth runestone, Hagalaz—hail—a stone that caused mayhem and disruption. It was a call to change within the lack of control it created.

And that was how he felt now. Out of control. Not of his lands and people, but of his life and of his destiny.

Hagalaz wasn't a bad rune. It gave the opportunity for a reset to true values when the truth had become blurred.

And his truth *had* become blurred. His family was either dead or gone—his child was still his family, just too young to be what he was looking for—and despite being surrounded by the good people of Drangar, he was alone.

He supped his mead and wished he knew what to do to shake his grief and lethargy. Right now, he was not a good king for his people.

He scrubbed his hand over his face before tugging at his beard and the small beads plaited into it. He should eat, but his appetite had left him.

Perhaps he would feel like eating in a while.

The pelting hail stopped as quickly as it had begun and he closed his eyes, resting his head back on the furs. His jaw ached from clenching his teeth and he tried to relax the best he could.

Soon his thoughts went to his twin brother. Haakon was always quick to smile, to help someone, to tell sagas to the children of the village. The opposite of Ravn, he knew that. It just wasn't in Ravn's nature to waste time on trivial pursuits or things that didn't benefit him directly.

And that streak in his nature had cost him a lot in his life. Luckily, Siggy had seen past it, to the person beneath his hard exterior. But no one else ever had.

Everyone else saw him as brittle, brackish, ambitious, and dogmatic. A man who decided on a goal and went for it, knocking everyone out of the way to get there.

Haakon's face still hovered in his mind. An image from the moment when he'd been on the ground, beaten, with Ravn's dagger aimed at his chest and ready to drive into his heart.

His eyes had flashed with sadness—sadness that the brother with whom he'd shared a womb had been about to take the life they'd started out on together.

Remorse tore through Ravn. He'd been so determined to be king, his ambition a real living creature inside of him, that he'd been ready to take the life of the one person who had always had his back. The brother he could rely on for anything. A man who had morals and love in his core and didn't deserve to die.

Thank goodness their father, Urd, had stopped him from carrying out the murder he'd been about to commit all in the name of a crown.

He opened his eyes, walked to the table, and poured more mead. A sudden pang hit him. He missed his brother.

He missed Astrid and Orm, too, even though they were annoying and whimsical in that order.

They were his kin. And he didn't even know where they were.

After taking a few big gulps of his drink, he walked to a carving on the wall. It was of a longboat with a great curled bow in the shape of a snake's head. Oars stuck from the sides, dipping into neat, semicircle waves. A line of shields ran the length of the boat and a sail puffed out above. It reminded him of the new boat Tyr had recently completed. A fine vessel that had yet to make its maiden voyage.

A noise to his right caught his attention. He frowned. What was it?

And then he saw that one of the apples he'd laid out for Thor had rolled clean off the wooden plinth and onto the floor, where it had stopped beside a table holding his sun-shadow board. Inherited from his father, it was a device for navigating the high seas.

His breath caught in his throat and he set down his drink. Was this a sign from the gods? From Thor himself?

A sign that he should travel on the very boat he was thinking of to find his siblings?

His heart rate picked up and with it, a spark of hope, a nugget of ambition again. Did Thor want him to set out on a quest to find Haakon and heal the rifts he'd gorged so deep? Was there a space for Astrid and Orm in his life again?

"Thor. Wise one." He walked to the monument and rested his hands on the cool stone. "I believe you have told me what I must do. And I will do it. I will right my wrongs so that the gods put me back on the true path of my destiny. In your name, and in the name of the All Father, I will succeed. I will atone." His words were clipped and determined and he could almost smell the ocean and feel the rock of the boat beneath his feet.

Whatever it took, however far he must travel, whatever battles he must brave, it was time to move his life on and face the future as a man, a king, and a brother.

Knock. Knock. Knock.

The gentle sound on the door wasn't the wind and Ravn turned to it. "Enter." He glanced at the sleeping child in the cot.

Thormod didn't stir.

The door opened and Helga slipped in with her hood pulled up tight and snow covering her boots. She stamped on the straw covered floor and pushed back her hood. "Your Grace. I have come to check on Thormod."

"Come. Come." He gestured to his friend, who had now

become his child's caretaker. "Sit. I wish to speak with you."

She stepped into the warmth, pushing her hood from her head and letting her long, blonde hair tumble free.

"I have made a decision," he told her.

"You have, Your Grace?" Her eyes widened.

"*Ja*. And at the morrow, I will set my new plan in motion."

She sat on the chair next to his and held her palms to the fire. "And what is this grand plan? You appear excited about it."

He poured a horn of mead and passed it to her. "I am."

She sipped her drink and raised her eyebrows. "So? What is it?"

"Ah." He tapped the side of his nose and grinned. "That is for me to know and you must wait to find out."

"I am intrigued." She swiped her tongue over her lips and smiled at him, tipping her head so her hair fell over her right shoulder.

"Oh, but…" He frowned, knowing he'd raised her hopes. "I am not going to make you my queen. Do not think that, Helga."

A flash of disappointment crossed her eyes and she quickly looked away, staring at the fire.

"I am sorry." He was only half sorry because she might as well know she wasn't queen material. He had no intention of ever marrying Helga despite their closeness.

"It is your prerogative as king," she said, "to choose a wife. A wife you think will make a wise and brave queen and if that is not me, then I understand. My blood is not royal and if it is the gods' bidding that it never is, I will accept my destiny."

"Mmm." He hesitated, trying to think what Haakon might say in this situation. He was much better with words that dealt with emotions. "I know you've held my hand and wiped my tears these last months, and I thank you."

She huffed out a breath. "I have never seen a tear, Your Grace, and I've held your cock as much as your hand."

He shrugged. Perhaps sentiment didn't suit him, after all. "That is probably true."

"It is how I have seen it." She took a drink then leaned forward and tore off a piece of bread. "How is Thormod today?"

"He has cried for his mother. His tears seem endless."

"Poor little thing." She looked into the quiet shadows. "It will take time; that is what heals."

"But if that is the case, I fear he will forget her eventually. I fear I will too." He frowned and summoned Siggy's pretty face with her eyes as blue as a summer's day and her lips soft and kissable and always ready to smile. He'd been a lucky man.

But she was gone now.

The same as everyone else.

"The gods have been harsh to you, but you still have your son—you must be thankful for that," Helga said softly.

"I am." He pressed his hand to his heart. "But he reminds me of everything I have lost."

She finished her food and drink and slipped to the floor at his side, legs folded and her hands on his thighs. She looked up at him, the light from the flames dancing on her face. "Some things that are lost can be found." She studied his eyes. "Is that what your new plan is? To go looking…for them?"

He laughed, not with much humor, but at least it was a change from scowling. "How is it you know me so well?"

"I have known you since we were each no taller than a goat and our pleasures came from poking at the fish in the creek, gathering smooth stones from the beach, and tormenting the frogs when they leaped from the spring water beside the well."

"*Ja*, we have been there for each other for many summers and winters. You should know that I will not desert you or my people for long. I wish for health and prosperity and new trading routes and partners."

"That is good to hear." She nodded and then tipped her head, studied him. "We have been there for each other even more so this winter."

He took a sip of his drink and listened to a roll of thunder in the distance. It was true. Helga had been a comfort to him since he'd lost Siggy. She always seemed to be there when his mood was nudging toward black. "Our pleasures are different now we are no longer children."

"They are, Your Grace."

He watched her mouth moving as she spoke.

"Would you like pleasure now?" She glanced downward, at his lap, as though seeing his cock through his clothing.

He swallowed as a rush of heat went to his groin. "*Ja.*"

"Then let me give it to you." She ran her palms up his thighs and tickled her fingers over him, stroking his now-stiffening cock.

Her mouth on him would be a balm for his pain and a welcome distraction from his grief. "Even though I will not make you queen?" He stroked her hair. "You still…?"

"*Ja*, for I am here to serve you, my king, and help you in any way I can." She pulled at his pants.

He lifted up so she could free his cock.

She gave him a sultry smile and licked her lips. And then her hands were on him, stroking him just the way he liked, firm and slow with her thumb smoothing around his tip.

He sighed and rested his head back, closing his eyes.

After a flick of her tongue, warm heat enveloped his shaft and he slipped his fingers into her silky hair.

Quickly, he reached full hardness and his balls tingled. She was good at this, her lips taut and her fingers busy, even though there was no emotion there, the act verging on hollow because he knew he'd never love her truly and deeply.

He groaned as his belly tightened. But he was in no rush. The dark night was long and his own thoughts monotonous.

"*Ja*, like that," he said on an exhalation. "Keep going."

She didn't answer, just kept adoring him with her mouth, unhurriedly pushing him toward a climax that he knew would be intense and fulfilling in a physical sense, if not an emotional one.

And then…then he would start planning his travels west.

Chapter Two

CARMEL FROWNED AT the Viking carefully stacking logs onto the fire in the center of his small, round dwelling. He was tall and his limbs rangy. His hair was long and wavy and tucked behind his ears. His angular face was streaked with the black kohl he'd swiped thickly beneath his eyes and he wore a necklace with a steel pendant shaped into what appeared to be a hammer.

"Do not fear. You will not be cold." He twitched his eyebrows and grinned. "I like to keep a fire burning, even here in Lothlend, where the earth is not so frozen as it is in my northern lands."

She didn't answer, just glared down at the chain between her ankles. He'd fastened the metal cuffs to her lower legs and a short length of chain between them meant she could only take half a step with each pace. Walking was awkward. Running impossible.

Which of course was his intention.

He wanted her to stay at his side… as his slave.

"I would rather freeze to death," she said, wrinkling her nose, "than have to see out the winter here with a heathen like you."

He chuckled. "I would not let you go to your heaven, Princess, because then who would wash my clothes, cook my food, and rub my back when it aches from chopping wood?"

"Exactly. I am a princess. You should treat me with respect and let me go home to my people."

"Oh, no, no, no." He shook his head. "I will not let you go. And do not think you can escape, either." With a stick, he poked at the glowing embers around the new logs. "You are staying here as my thrall." He pressed his free hand to his chest. "As my slave, you should be honored. I am Orm, the brother of the king."

"Ha, he is not a true king." Disgust twisted her mouth. "He is a Norseman who has no right to be here, no right to this land, no right to a crown or the attention of God."

"That is what you believe." Orm pointed at her with the stick he'd been poking the fire with. "But not what everyone else in Tillicoulty believes."

"If they consider themselves to be God-fearing Christians, then they would denounce him."

"Ah, but King Haakon *is* a Christian. He was baptized, you know."

Carmel was quiet for a moment, then, "I don't believe you." She folded her arms. "He wouldn't forsake his own gods."

"I speak the truth. His wife, Queen Kenna, insisted on it before they were wed. The priest Olaf performed the ceremony himself. I was a witness to the event."

Her scowl deepened. "That one act does not make him Christian. He must follow Jesus and have God in his heart. He must learn the scriptures of the Holy Bible and renounce all sins, act only with love and compassion."

"The way your father did when he collected taxes from these people, who already had so little?"

"The taxes were just and due." She bristled. Somewhere deep inside, she knew there was some truth to Orm's words.

"'Just'?" Orm laughed. "'Due'?"

His cackle grated on her. It was high-pitched and somewhat manic.

"Aye, they were just taxes for hunting and fishing on my father's land."

"It was *not* your father's land." His mirth stopped abruptly and he leaned forward, his dark eyes flashing. "It was and still is the land of the people who farm it, who know and respect it, whose ancestors have lived here since the great world serpent,

Jörmungandr, took his tail into his mouth and created the Earth. Your father had no claim to it and no right to charge tax." He shrugged. "And now he will never collect again."

A pang of grief twisted Carmel's heart. Her father had been power-hungry, it was true, but nowhere near as brutally ambitious as the heathen Vikings, and no matter any of his faults, he had still been her father and she'd known he'd loved her, as she'd loved him. "You are a monster." She pursed her lips and looked away from him, staring pointedly at the small cot in the corner in which she'd spent the night before.

"*Ja*, that is right." He cupped her chin and turned her to face him. "I am a monster, the monster from all of your worst nightmares, and now you are mine. You belong to the monster. Princess Carmel is now Thrall Carmel, my slave."

"You think you are so powerful," she said, glaring at him, "but never forget power wields enemies."

"That is right! You are right!" He released her chin, roughly pushing at her face. "And we will be ready for them, for did you not see our victory? Did you not witness how your father fared when he declared war upon us?" He made a slashing motion over his throat and his eyes flashed.

"Holy Mother of Jesus." She crossed herself. "You know no mercy. Your wickedness is every bit as heinous as your reputation said it would be."

"You had better believe it." He laughed and stood, pouring ale from a casket.

"I wish to go to church." She pushed to standing. "I know you have one in Tillicoulty. I have seen it."

"It is not mine."

She said nothing.

"What use is one god? I have many." He pinched the small hammer that sat just below his throat. "And one day, I will sup with them in Valhalla and regale them with my stories. Stories of adventure and travel, victory and pleasure…and of a thrall princess I claimed as my own."

"It is a truth, as I see it, that you cannot claim a woman as a wife, which is why you are so pleased to have claimed me despite my unwillingness. I am a woman who has no choice but to be at your side because you have made me all but lame." She lifted her right foot, jangling the chain. "Never forget, I am not here by choice. That should make you uncomfortable at best, terrified at worst. Each night when you close your eyes and your guard is down, there is no knowing what I will do. I almost killed one of yours, remember, with a spear to the head."

He scowled at her, two deep lines on his forehead, as he drank deep. "*Almost*, for you are no warrior." He spat on the floor.

"I am going to pray." Carmel shriveled her nose then took small steps across the dwelling to the doorway. It was slow progress. Each time the chain became taut, she nearly toppled over.

"All Father, give me strength," he muttered, tossing his empty mug to one side.

"Oh!" The next thing she knew, she was in the air, folded in half over his shoulder again with his hand slapped against her ass. "Put me down."

"I cannot stand and watch your ridiculous shuffle all the way to the church." He headed out into the open and stood tall as he strode past a pigpen, his feet sinking into a muddy patch of earth. "I will carry you there."

"I would… rather walk." Each step he took seized the air from her lungs. "Even if it… takes me… all day."

"You do not get to decide."

Her hair fell forward and shame washed over her as she heard voices—familiar voices that spoke with her Lothlend accent, not the strange gruffness of the Vikings. Surely, someone would help her? She was their princess. For years, they had bowed down to her family.

But as they neared the church, she heard nothing but chuckles of amusement at her predicament and one gruff comment about her having a nice ass. Hope was futile—at least the hope that the people of Tillicoulty would help her.

Hell, right now, her father's head and those of his men's were up on stakes at the entrance to the fortified village as a warning to others.

These people had changed.

And it was all because of their new Norse leader, Haakon.

"I said, *put me down*." She kicked her feet and gripped Orm's belt.

Suddenly, she was being upended and the soles of her boots hit the ground. For a moment, she was dizzy and closed her eyes, the stone slab beneath her swaying.

"You are here," he said, pointing at the tiny church.

It had a small steeple with likely one miniscule bell to call for prayers, a single cross-shaped window, and an oak door that had a split in it along with rusting iron hinges.

She brushed down her gown then tightened the belt at her waist, which fastened her thick, woolen cape securely to her body.

"I suppose if your people hadn't had to pay taxes, it would be a better temple, *ja?*"

"It is not a cathedral, that is true. But why would they need one?" A pang of guilt hit her. It really was in a bedraggled state for a holy building.

He shrugged and ran his hand through his hair. It instantly fell messily around his face again. His jawline was smooth and strong and his nose dead straight.

"How come you speak my language?" she asked suddenly.

"Joseph."

"Who is Joseph? And not the one from the Bible—I know who he is."

"I only know one Joseph." Orm shrugged again. "A thrall my father took from a monastery during one of his first sailings west. He has been with our family for many years." He drew a circle like a halo over the top of his head. "His hair grew back and he learned our ways, even became a fighter when he had to be."

"He went... Your father took him to *your* lands?" Was this true?

"*Ja*, he captured him the way I have captured you. Which meant that Joseph was no longer a free man. He had to go where my father, King of Drangar, wanted him to go. And that was to serve our family for the rest of his days."

Her mouth fell open. Was that to be her fate? Serving this wicked, excitable, unpredictable Viking until she was an old lady? And if so, would he bundle her onto a boat and take her across the seas to lands unknown?

She kissed the cross at her neck and stepped away from him, toward the church door. If ever there was a time she needed her prayers to be heard, it was now. She would kneel before whatever meager altar there was and pray for her father's soul and for her own future.

"Hey, Orm." A deep voice to her right.

"*Ja?*" her capturer answered.

"We are preparing Egil's pyre at the beach. Come and help us."

Carmel hurried toward the church as best she could, her heart thumping. Would he stop her going to pray? It was the only thing she could do right now to soothe her soul.

"Princess," he called at her back.

She didn't pause. The church was only a few steps away. It was a refuge, a house of safety. At least in her mind, it felt that way.

"I will return for you here. Do not try and escape. The good people of Tillicoulty will not allow you through the fort entrance, but if you did slip through, know that the wolves would eat you alive. The scent of blood on the battlefield has brought them from the forest, salivating, stomachs rumbling, hunting for leftover guts and brains. Your god will not save you from their jaws and you have no hope of running away from them."

She didn't answer. Instead, she pushed into the small, dark

church and dashed at the tears slipping wetly down her cheeks.

The silence wrapped around her like a heavy cloak and she waited for her eyes to adjust to the dim lighting.

A single tallow candle was lit on a table beneath the cross window. Next to it, a crude, wooden cross sat on a piece of clean linen. There was no Bible to read, no gold or incense. It was a truly humble church with little of the spoils of wealth she'd heard filled the house of God in Rome.

But it was a church, and she was alone for the first time in days.

She moved past the pews, rubbing her hands together against the cold, then came to a halt at the altar. A small, dusty red rug was on the floor and she folded down onto it, hands in prayer, eyes closed.

Her father's face was the first thing that came to mind and she thanked God it was an image of him smiling and not beheaded. But still, the tears fell. Still, her heart broke.

She thought of her mother. She wouldn't know her husband's fate yet. That she was a widow, a queen without a king. It would take days for any survivors of the battle to journey west with news. And poor Alfred, her young brother, he was now fatherless and a king at such a young age.

And then, she prayed, rescue would come. Surely, her mother would gather a group of brave soldiers to rescue her only daughter from the heinous Vikings who had invaded their land.

"God Almighty, please hear my prayers and deliver me from this barbaric monster. Either save me and send me swiftly home or take me in my sleep before he rapes and murders me." She paused to sniff and swipe her upper lip. "I trust in you. My faith is unwavering, oh, mighty—"

"They are not all bad, you know."

She startled and spun around.

An older man with a long, white beard stood in the entrance. He held what appeared to be a Bible.

"Who are you?"

"I am Olaf of Tillicoulty."

"Are you the priest?"

"I am the nearest thing our community has." He smiled and walked forward. "When the Irish priest left, he entrusted me with the Holy Book and the souls of our village."

"A great responsibility." She stood, wary of a local who had become convinced that letting a Viking king rule was acceptable.

"One that I am honored to receive." He came closer and crossed himself before the candle.

"How can you…?" She gestured at the door. "How can you all just let them settle here? They have more than put their heathen feet beneath the table, they have deigned it appropriate to rule and you have let them." She shook her head.

"They didn't give us much choice, if you must know."

"There is always choice."

"Not if you want to live." He looked her up and down. "Surely, you must understand that, given your current predicament."

She scowled and folded her arms. "He is a madman, the one who thinks I am some kind of possession he can just take."

Olaf nodded slowly. "Orm is…interesting."

She huffed. "Interesting, if you consider that word to mean *crazed, volatile, dogmatic, and blasphemous.*"

"It is true, he is all of those things." He shrugged and his mouth downturned.

"And his face." Again, she wiped at her damp cheeks. "He makes himself look all the crazier with the kohl beneath his eyes."

"It is his way. I have become used to it. He has never hurt anyone in the village, even when he did not agree with his brother becoming Christian."

"So it is true."

"That King Haakon is one of the Good Lord's flock? Aye, it is."

"Good, for that means he will have to answer at the gates of heaven, to Saint Peter himself, about the cruel end he bestowed upon my father."

"Aye, that could have been more dignified."

She stared at him, mouth open.

"I guess our king was simply making a point. That Tillicoulty is a new kingdom and not one to be poked."

"'*Poked*'? How can you stand it? These people have taken over."

"And for the better. For now, we do not have to pay unjust taxes. Now we can farm and work our land and keep the fruits of our labor. Your father worked not a day in our fields. Why should he be rewarded?"

"It is the way of the world." Again, she bristled with an uneasy feeling floating in her stomach. Was it right just because it had always been? She wasn't sure.

"It is not the way of our world anymore." Olaf stood and came close, gently resting his arthritic hand on her shoulder. "You should accept, Princess Carmel, that your life has changed drastically. It is turned upon its head. No longer are you a free woman of privilege. You are a captive of the Vikings. But…" He paused. "Play the game well and you could have a happier future."

"I doubt it." She glared at him. "And when my mother, the queen, sends help my way you will not be spared, Priest, for you are in cahoots with the Norsemen. You have been weak and traitorous allowing them to pitch here, sleep with your women, control your borders. You will not be spared."

"That may be." He smiled, just a little. "But your rescuers will have to get past our defenses first. As you may have noticed, they are quite impressive."

Carmel resisted stamping her foot. "We'll have to wait and see who is right, Priest."

$$\succ\!\!\bullet\!\!\bullet\!\!-\!\!-\!\!-\!\!\circ\!\!-\!\!-\!\!-\!\!\bullet\!\!\bullet\!\!\prec$$

Chapter Three

"THRALL, GET HERE!"

Carmel turned to the church door. It was flung open and Orm stood there, his hands on his hips and his frame in silhouette.

"What?" She frowned at him.

"We are going to the beach. Our fallen warrior friend Egil is to be sent out to sea right now."

"May God bless his soul." Olaf crossed himself and sent his eyes heavenward.

"What are you doing?" she said to the old man. "He was a heathen and a murderer."

"He died defending Tillicoulty and the good men, women, and children who live here. Egil deserves God's mercy and eternal salvation."

She huffed and pushed past him, making her way down the aisle in her strange, frustrating shuffle.

"Take these off," she said, kicking her left leg up to shake her bonds. "How can I walk to the beach?" She glared at Orm. He'd covered the top half of his face entirely in black soot that made him look even more demonic.

He grinned. "Did you pray for them to come off?"

"Well… I… No… But I had other things to pray for, like you dropping dead."

He laughed, showing big, white teeth that matched the whites of his eyes. "Well, I will be dead one day, so that prayer will be answered, but if you did not pray for your chains to be gone, then how can it happen? That is how your god works, right?"

"You have no idea." She pursed her lips.

"Come. I will carry you."

"No… Get off… I…"

But instead of throwing her over his shoulder, this time, he scooped her into his arms and she had no choice but to cling to his shoulder with one hand and wrap her arm around his neck.

Being so close to him was repulsive. He smelled of leather and soap and perhaps rosemary too.

A procession was heading toward the beach and they joined it. A lone gull called mournfully overhead and the briny scent of the ocean caught on a stiff breeze.

Haakon and his wife walked hand in hand, her scarlet gown long and made of quality material. His fur was thick and sumptuous and his hair braided tightly down the back of his head.

Beside them stood another couple, both with hair the color of the brightest orange sunset. He leaned to speak to her as they walked, his hand touching the small of her back. Carmel recognized him as the tall man she'd made good aim at with her spear and her as the woman who had been itching to kill her when she'd first been captured.

Perhaps she'd have been better off if she were dead rather than here.

As they walked along the small path through the dunes, wispy grass bending in the wind, she saw the horizon was heavy with blackening clouds. There'd be snow soon, she was sure of it, and the churned earth of the battlefield would freeze.

A small pier led out to sea, the waves frothing and fizzing against its timber supports. On the left of it were two small fishing boats anchored with thick rope. On the right was a wooden raft piled high with dry wood. Atop it a body, Egil, and around him furs, mistletoe sprigs and armor set out neatly.

"What is that?" she asked Orm when he set her down on the

beach.

"A burial pyre. Egil will need those things in his next life. His armor, his cloak and arm ring, his tankard for supping with the gods in the Great Hall."

"It will all be burned?"

"*Ja*, the flames will take it with him to Valhalla." His hair lifted on the wind. "Sit. Sit beside me." He dropped to the ground and folded his legs, picking up two sticks. He banged on a skin drum, quickly setting up a rhythm that vibrated through her like a heartbeat.

A gust of wind pressed her cape to her legs and nipped her cheeks. She sat, taking some shelter from his body. Kenna, the queen, lit iron baskets along the pier and they burst to life, adding color to the gray sky.

The crowd huddled closer, their faces somber, as Haakon lifted the flaming torch.

"Good people of Tillicoulty, today we honor our dead. Those in the churchyard and those, like Egil son of Daneson of Drangar, who take a different route to their eternal life." He paused and surveyed the villagers. "To die in battle is to die with honor. It is to die leaving a legacy on Earth that your memory will never fade. To die for a cause, a belief, is to die for a reason and there is no greater reason that freedom." He shouted the last word.

A cheer went up.

"And as my friend, the priest Olaf, has committed Christian bodies to God, I now commit Egil to the gods who await him in Valhalla." He raised his head, flashing his thick chin and neck tattoo. "Feast well, my friend. Feast well." He held the torch aloft.

Suddenly, the woman with flame-red hair sprang forward and snatched the torch from him. A frown slashed over her brow and she stepped up to the pyre, holding it at the ready.

The king scowled and marched up to her. An argument ensued. Carmel was too far away to hear what they were saying. But what she couldn't understand was why a king was letting a woman create such a scene—more than a scene. After a few minutes, she appeared to win the argument and Haakon stepped back.

She held the torch over the raft, the wind whipping her hair around her face. "Hail to the gods. Hail to the dead! Hail to the kinsmen, the family, the shields, and the swords. Long may Egil's memory live in the minds of the living and his bravery and wisdom by rejoiced as he sits in the mighty halls of Valhalla."

She tossed the torch onto the body.

Instantly, the mistletoe leaped into flame. Three others who could only be Norsemen released the ropes and gave the raft a shove out into the tide.

The current caught it immediately, bobbing it this way and that as flames licked upward, eager to devour their feast.

"Look!" The queen stepped forward, pointing east of the pyre raft. "Someone is coming our way."

Carmel peered forward—it seemed everybody's attention went to the horizon. Orm beat the drum faster, the boom deafening, as though he were excited by the sudden appearance of a boat. It was a Viking longboat; she'd seen enough of them to know that. The curled bow was unmistakable and this one appeared to have been carved like a serpent with a long, forked tongue. A tall, bearded man stood at the prow, arm curled around the serpent's neck as he shielded his eyes, peering forward.

Suddenly, Orm threw his drumsticks to the sand. He then leaped up and ran toward the pier. The crowd parted to let him through—if they hadn't, he'd have run straight through them. "Thor's thunder rumbles around a crown!" he shouted. "It rumbles and it strikes with lightning…and here is the lightning."

Carmel had no idea what was going on. As Egil's body drifted out to sea ablaze and with all of his worldly possessions, another boat was making dock against the pier. What she did know was that whoever it was, it had shocked Orm, the king, and the woman with the red hair.

Who could it be?

The new arrival leaped off, his white fur cloak flying out

behind him. His hair was long but plaited neatly against his head and his beard was thick and shiny and dotted with beads. His boots landed with a *whump.*

Orm was practically dancing around him, his arms waving in the air as he let out whoops of anticipation.

Carmel stood and glanced at the dunes. Should she make a run for it now that everyone was distracted by this new and unexpected visitor? From here, she wouldn't have the fort walls or the watchman to contend with.

Just the wolves.

And the bloody battlefield complete with heads on stakes.

A shiver went through her that had nothing to do with the cold.

"Who could it be?" a woman, petite and with dark-brown hair, said at Carmel's side.

"You tell me. *You* live here," Carmel snapped.

"I have never seen him before. This is only the second Norse ship to come to our shores. Usually, they go straight past us, to richer lands. We have little to raid here."

"I have noticed."

The woman smiled. "I am Anna. My father is Hywel, the carpenter. You might have seen him helping build the funeral pyre."

"No, I didn't see. I was praying."

"As would I in your position."

Carmel peered closer at the young woman. Perhaps she would be sympathetic, help her escape and provide her with the tools she'd need to survive. "Prayers are all I can rely on." She paused. "I have a monster controlling me, the devil himself."

She laughed. "Orm is not the devil."

"Are we looking at the same man?" Carmel asked incredulously as she flung her hand in his direction.

"Oh, he's excitable and he thinks differently to other people, but he has a good heart."

"You call this having a good heart?" She raised her gown to

show the chain between her ankles.

"Well, at least he isn't planning on spreading your legs." Anna raised her eyebrows.

"What? I…" Carmel shook her head to rid the image of Orm forcing himself on her, taking her maidenhood. Just the thought made her stomach churn.

"Come on. Let us go and see what is happening." Anna held out her arm. "I will help you walk."

Carmel said nothing, but she did take the offered support and together, they made their way over the sand to the pier. When they drew closer, she could hear the conversation between the king and the new arrival.

"Ravn, I didn't expect to see you again in this life." Haakon tipped his chin and puffed up his chest.

The tall stranger withdrew his sword from his belt and it glinted against the steely sky. He then lay it down with a flourish and held up his palms. "I have not come to wield weapons, brother. I have come in peace."

"Is that so?" Haakon placed his hands on his hips, spreading his cloak out like wings and showcasing the sword, axe, and dagger on his belt. He made no move to lay down arms.

"Aye, I am here to make amends." Ravn's voice was deep and hoarse, as though the salt from the ocean had scratched his throat after many days of traveling.

The woman with the red hair slapped her thigh and laughed, but not with humor. "*Amends!* You are too late. Those bridges are burned."

"Astrid." He stepped forward, hand held out, fist tight. "This is for you."

With a frown, she took it. "What is it?"

"Look."

She opened her hand then snatched it closed again. She drew the object to her chest.

Carmel couldn't see what it was, but it had certainly had an effect on the woman they called "Astrid." Her mouth flattened and she turned away to face the tall man with one arm in a sling.

His face was deathly serious as he studied first her and then directed his attention at the newcomer. "What did you give her?"

"It is what was in our father's hand when I found him dead in his bed at the beginning of a new moon."

"'Dead'?" Haakon echoed with a frown. "Our father is dead?"

Kenna put her hand on her husband's upper arm, a soothing gesture.

"You're lying," Orm said, flapping around. "Lies spill from your mouth."

"I am telling the truth," Ravn said. "He went to the gods without battle and without a goodbye." He paused. "His heart broke without you all. I was not enough."

Astrid seemed to slump. It was the first time Carmel had seen her looking anything other than fierce and battle-ready.

The man at her side wrapped his arm around her shoulders and drew her close, murmuring something in her ear. She softened against him, her face hidden.

"I think it is the king's brother," Anna said quietly, "who has arrived on our shores."

Carmel was still studying the newcomer. His sudden presence had certainly caused a stir and Orm was more fractious than ever.

Ravn looked around. His attention settled on the three Vikings standing on the pier glowering at him. "I am sorry for your loss. Egil was a good man."

"He was," the tallest muttered. "And now he sups with the gods and beds as many virgins as he wishes."

"What happened to him?" Ravn turned to Haakon.

"The Valkyrie came for him."

"He died in battle?"

"*Ja.*"

"What battle?"

"Come, get your men from the boat." Haakon looked down at the weapons. "If you have truly come peacefully, I will feed you before you go on your way." He gave a last look out to sea.

The pyre was way out in the distance, only a small glow now, and he raised one hand before turning away from it.

"Thrall. Thrall. Come with me."

Suddenly, Orm was before her, bouncing like an excited puppy. "You have much work to do. You must serve the king and his brother, also a king. You are indeed privileged to have such a duty."

"I will send my thanks to God," she muttered.

"Anna," Orm said, reaching for Anna's hand and drawing her knuckles to his mouth. "My sweet Anna, will you ensure my thrall goes to the Great House and then show her where the heather ale and the ham are? We will feast and regale each other with sagas of battles and of our father until late into the night."

"I am sorry," Anna said. "About your father, Orm." A line formed between her eyebrows.

"Do not be sorry. He lived a good long life and now is with the gods, who always looked upon him favorably. Well, they did until I refused to be a sacrifice at Uppsalla." He cackled. "But who is laughing now? I am here to feast in our new kingdom and he is not." He clapped and spun around, racing back to his brothers and sister with sand kicking up behind him.

"I have never met anyone like him," Carmel said with a frown.

"Neither have I." Anna sighed. "Come, the snow is about to fall."

As she'd spoken, a fat, white flake floated down. It matched the new arrival's cloak and a tremble went through her as she thought of the size and strength of his Viking body beneath those layers of clothes.

Chapter Four

Soon, Carmel was in the warmth of the Great House. A big, round dwelling that appeared to have one large bedroom with a fire at the back and the rest used as a meeting place with a fire trough, flame baskets, and a banquet table. Two large chairs sat the head, sealskins hung around drying, and the walls were adorned with wooden crosses, antlers, sprigs of pheasant feathers, and bundles of drying herbs. Several barrels of ale were set in the corner.

"It's warm in here," Anna said. "Better for you."

"Why are you being kind to me?" Carmel asked. "I'm a prisoner. I was fighting your people yesterday."

"You are a fellow Christian and woman of Lothlend." She nodded at the cross that hung from a hoop in Carmel's ear—a gift from her father on her thirteenth summer.

"That is true."

"And God says we must be merciful and find forgiveness in our hearts." She touched the cross. "Don't you agree?"

"Aye, I guess I do." Carmel shuffled to the barrels and began to fill jugs with the frothy, sweet-smelling liquid. "The woman with the red hair who lit the pyre. Tell me about her."

"She is the king's sister. Her name is Astrid and she has been gone for weeks, only just returned with news of your father's army approaching."

Ah, so that is why Tillicoulty had been prepared for their attack. They'd been seen camping in the valley. It made sense to

Carmel now.

"And the man, with the red hair, he is the queen's brother, Hamish," Anna went on. "He disappeared at the same time as Astrid. Bryce—that's our friend—and I, we guessed he had gone to Astrid. Ever since she arrived he had this stupid soppy look in his eyes whenever she was around."

"From what I've seen, she doesn't exactly exude gentleness and forgiveness."

"You're right." Anna set out a plate of ham then reached for bread and a knife. "She is a shield-maiden. Skilled and brave. She taught us to fight the best she could in the time we had before your army arrived."

Carmel nodded, preferring not to remember the carnage that she'd been forced to join in with, even though she was not a warrior—the screams of agony as the spiked fence had been brought up on charging men. The dirty ditch that had been a trap and left them with no hope as spears and swords were driven downward. The heads on spikes beside the watchtower.

"How did you find out about King Haakon?" Anna asked.

"A wanderer." Carmel shuffled to an ale barrel and began filling tankards with the cloudy liquid.

"He'd been to Tillicoulty?" Anna carved the bread.

"Spoken to the king himself. Or so he said."

"Do you recall his name?"

Carmel shook her head and pointed to her eye. "He wore a patch here. He swore he had told the king nothing of import and instead came straight to us to tell us my father had been usurped."

Anna huffed. "I am sure he was well rewarded for his loyalty to King Athol. Though wanderers care only for themselves, despite what yarns they spin."

Carmel agreed; that had always been her experience.

A sudden bang and gush of leaf-strewn wind announced the arrival of the King Haakon, his men, and his brother. Behind Ravn was a gaggle of weary seafarers with wide curious eyes and bedraggled clothing and beards.

"These men are hungry!" Haakon shouted. "Ensure the feast is plentiful and the ale flows as though Aegir himself were partying with us." He took a seat on the big chair, his wife sitting next to him.

Even though she had not been queen long, Kenna had a regal tilt to her chin and her eyes sparkled with intelligence. She was studying the king's brother Ravn with intense curiosity. When a small barn owl flew from the rafters and sat on a perch close to her shoulder, she took no notice, such was her interest.

"You have finally taken a wife," Ravn said, holding up a horn of wine as though toasting Kenna.

"She is the only woman for me," said Haakon, his eyes growing soft. "The gods mapped out our destiny many years ago and I should thank you for sending me to her."

"Thank me?" Ravn sat on a bench, legs wide, one elbow on a table just behind him and looking very much as though he were settling in for a long conversation.

"*Ja.*" Haakon narrowed his eyes. "If you had not become consumed in your quest for power, brother. If you had not tried to kill me with a dagger through my heart, I would never have traveled west that day. I would never have washed up on these shores and stared up into the face of a goddess."

Ravn shifted his weight and took a drink.

"My very own living Valkyrie." Haakon took Kenna's hand and kissed her knuckles. "More beautiful than I could ever have dreamed of."

"It is an honor to meet you, Queen Kenna," Ravn said.

"You tried to kill my husband. I never thought I would meet you." She held his eye contact and bit on her bottom lip. "I'm not sure how I feel about you on our lands, in our home."

"But I *didn't* kill him," Ravn said. "I could have, but I was merciful."

"Only because Father intervened." Orm took a mug of ale from Carmel and used it to point at Ravn. "You had murder in your eyes. You wanted the spill of blood."

"I believed it was the gods' will," Ravn said. "Now I understand that it was not."

"How?" Astrid sat on Hamish's lap and looped an arm around his neck. "How do you know that now?"

"Ah." Ravn tapped the side of his nose. "You, dear sister, helped me with that."

She frowned. "I wasn't even there."

"But you had been. On that last day in Uppsalla, you read my runestones, remember?"

She tilted her head. "Go on."

"And you threw Laguz for me."

She didn't reply.

Ravn leaned forward and tugged at one of the beads plaited into his beard. He had the exact same profile as his brother. Heavy brow; long, strong nose; and neck thick with muscle. But there was something wilder about him. Maybe it was because he was, in theory, amongst enemies, family enemies, but still, it certainly sounded like the last time the siblings had been together, tensions had been running high.

"The water rune," Ravn went on, "showing me a reflection of myself. I liked what I saw because I saw a king, a man of great power, a husband, and a father to a son who would become my heir."

"Why did the meaning of Laguz change for you?" Hamish asked. "It sounds to me it was reversed."

"What do you know of runestones, Christian?" one of Ravn's men snapped as he squared his shoulders.

Hamish shrugged and held the man's gaze. "I have learned."

"Laguz prompted you to look into the darkness of your unconscious," Astrid nodded. "Deep into the shadows."

"I saw darkness." Ravn looked around at the rapt faces. For a moment, his attention landed on Carmel, his piercing, glacier-blue eyes drilling into her before moving back to Haakon. "What I'd failed to see was that my twin brother and I had become as opposite as day and night, as different as summer and winter. He was the light and I was the darkness."

Haakon frowned and leaned forward, forearms on his thighs, hands dangling.

"And I didn't like that. The gods didn't like it," Ravn continued. "And I paid for it, not just with the loss of Father, but Siggy and our unborn child were also taken."

Haakon frowned. "I am sorry to hear that."

Ravn's jaw tensed. It was clearly a loss that pained him.

For a moment, Carmel almost felt sorry for him. Then she remembered her own losses and how much she hated the Vikings and their murderous, heathen customs.

"I had lost my way, lost control of my destiny." Ravn popped a chunk of ham into his mouth and chewed. "And I wanted to reset, rebalance. I wanted to find my family."

Orm let out a sudden huge roar of laughter and clutched his belly.

Carmel shrank back into the shadows, standing slightly behind Anna.

"You wanted to find your family? How? You didn't even know where we were," Orm said.

"I am here, aren't I?" Ravn didn't seem remotely perturbed by Orm's wild laughter.

"But how?" Kenna asked, holding out her arm for the owl to hop onto. She fed it a morsel of ham.

"It is the will of the gods," Ravn said. "It is the true path of my destiny." He stood and held out his mug. "And I am returned to it after veering off course for some time. Toast with me."

Anna nudged Carmel. "Fill his horn for him."

Quickly, Carmel lifted the earthenware jug and shuffled toward the towering Viking king. His fur cape was matted and his hair salt-sprinkled. He had ink below his right eye in the shape of a small star.

He frowned at her. "Why do you walk that way?"

Her jaw tensed and her heart thudded. The last thing she

wanted was to be the center of attention in a room full of foes.

"Woman," he snapped. "Why do you walk like that?"

She raised the muddy hem of her gown to show him the chain and ankle cuffs.

"You are a thrall?" He studied her closely, seeming to notice the cross hanging from her right ear.

"She is *my* thrall!" Orm leaped up and bounced toward her before circling with flamboyant hand gestures as though she were quite the prize. "I captured her in battle. She is a princess. My princess thrall. How lucky am I?"

"A princess?" Ravn said, peering even closer at her. "You are a princess?"

For a moment, she held his gaze, but then she quickly filled his mug and took a step backward. Being a slave was mortifying. Being a crazed Norseman's slave was more degrading and shameful than she could ever have believed possible.

She'd never felt further from being a princess in her life.

Her shoulder bumped into Anna's and she tucked behind her, using her new friend as a shield. It was all she had.

"Do not look at her like that," Orm said, holding up his pinkie finger. "As if you want to put your little cock inside her. She is my slave to do with what I wish."

Ravn frowned. "My cock is none of your business and it is not little."

"But *she* is." Orm pointed. "She is mine."

Oh, God. That was what he was planning? Fucking her? Forcing himself upon her? The thought was hideous and her stomach churned. It would have been better to have died in battle than live like this.

Ravn's eyes narrowed and he turned back to Haakon and sipped his ale. "I saw the pyre. We have stopped in three coves on our journey here. My plan was to search until I found my kin. But the pyre led me straight to you."

"Perthro," Astrid said suddenly. "That was one of the rune-stones that spoke that day. It signifies the mystery of the unknown and unknowable."

"*Ja.*" Ravn pointed at her. "And now I know. The funeral pyre gave me knowledge. It was fate that we sailed past on this day and saw it."

Haakon stood and placed his hands on his hips. He studied his brother. "It does seem as if it is Almighty God's will."

"'Almighty God's will'?" Ravn repeated with a scoff.

"*Ja.*" Haakon looked at two older men, villagers. "I am Christian now. These men can confirm it."

"You have denounced the gods!" Ravn jumped to his feet. "You are a traitor, brother, a traitor to Odin."

"Do you wish to fight again?" Haakon gripped the hilt of his sword. "I allowed you onto my land because you said you had come in peace."

"Before I knew you were Christian!"

Queen Kenna stood at her husband's side. The owl on her shoulder flapped its wings and let out a squawk. "My husband is a man of great depth," she said. "He is learning the Christian way, though it is hard for his heart to let go of the gods who have walked with him since the day he was born. Gods who are ruled by the greatest God." She touched her cross. "All the gods have been with him in battles and in storms, which is why he breathes this day and his heart beats. I understand that he pays his respects to them all."

Ravn flexed his fingers then drew them into a fist. "Father will be looking down on you with shame."

"Father had ambition for travel and learning and that is what I have done. I am walking in the footsteps he had hoped to tread himself." Haakon looked upward. "He will be smiling down on me, the gods at his side."

"This is how he is now." Astrid flung her arm toward Haakon and rolled her eyes. "It is easier to go along with it than fight his new, crazed ways."

"You have not forsaken the All Father, Astrid? Tell me you have not." Ravn spun to her.

"No! The gods and goddesses have not deserted me and I will not desert them."

Ravn looked at Orm.

Orm laughed and circled his finger beside his head as though spinning thoughts. He gave no answer.

Ravn sat with a sigh and reached for a slice of buttered bread. "What is the land like here?"

"It is good and fertile, not as frozen as the north, and there are crops we haven't seen." Haakon leaned forward, clearly warming to the new topic of conversation. "And taste good."

"Crops that grow all year," a huge Norseman added, his sudden input in a gruff voice making Carmel stare at him. The man was huge and he had discarded his tunic, as though hot, and his wide, broad chest was splattered with ink in a variety of complex roped designs that twisted and turned over his muscles and down to his belly.

"Who is that?" Carmel whispered to Anna.

"Gunner. He is one of them."

She had guessed that. He was unmistakably Viking.

"We are willing to teach you our farming ways, brother Ravn," Queen Kenna said. "My father, a village elder, is a generous man with knowledge." She pointed to a stooped man with a graying beard and a tasseled hood pulled up over his head. He was spooning broth into his mouth and appeared very relaxed—much more than anyone in her village would have been if Vikings had walked in and taken over.

These people were weak to be so easily invaded and to then be so accommodating. If she'd been feeling generous, she'd have thought they had an alternate plan and were playing a long game, but she didn't think that was the case. The Vikings were marrying their women and ruling their lands. The Tillicoulty people may as well have set an arrowed sign on the beach welcoming them in.

And Haakon being Christian now. That was ridiculous. It was clear his faith was still in the heathen gods, and his brother… Huh, he thought of nothing else.

Chapter Five

RAVN SLEPT ON a straw cot in the Great House. He was full of ale and food and it was a relief not to be on a rocking boat surrounded by the grunts and nocturnal stenches of his fellow travelers.

When he opened his eyes and saw sunlight sneaking in through cracks in the wood paneling, he let out a sigh. His plan to find his siblings had been vague and possibly foolhardy. After they'd left the fjord, he'd had no idea which direction they'd journeyed in. He'd guessed west, which had been Haakon's obsession—he'd long since bored of going east into the Baltic lands.

It was Njord himself who had sent Ravn south. He'd puffed up his cheeks and blown their sail straight into the cove his brother stood in, almost as if waiting for Ravn's arrival.

The gods worked in mysterious ways, for if Egil had not gone to sup with the gods, and his mortal body sent on its way that very day, Ravn would never have seen the plume of black smoke smudging the sky and the flames flashing as the funeral raft dipped and bobbed on the waves.

He'd been drawn to it in an instant. Knowing it was a sign. His men had rowed with fierce determination, no doubt hoping for the spoils of a raid and not believing, as Ravn had done, that he was about to find his brothers and sister.

He sat and rubbed his beard. His men were strewn around still sleeping in various states of undress and with a constant snoring rumble.

Standing, Ravn adjusted his pants and belt and searched for food and drink. He found ale and took a slug.

"Eggs."

He turned.

Queen Kenna stood in the doorway with a basket. She pushed her hood from her head and stomped her boots free of snow.

"An egg would be a treat after time at sea," he said.

"I will cook for you." She strode past him. Her pants were the same deep red as her gown had been the day before and her hair was plaited back over her head in several thin rows. She wore a cross at her neck.

"Where's Haakon?" he asked.

"He's with my father. They are discussing the crop field. The battle with King Athol has left damage. It must be repaired as soon as the weather allows."

"What is the weather like today? I can see sunlight."

"Aye, there is sun, more than where you are from." She smiled. "But the snow came again in the night. The ground is frozen once more, which will be a relief from the mud."

He sat and watched as she set a pan over the fire and began to crack eggs, whisking them with a spoon as she did so and then sprinkling in dried herbs.

"Why did you marry my brother?" he asked.

She looked up at him, surprise widening her eyes "Why not?"

"He invaded your village. Surely, he's your enemy."

She laughed. "It is true, he did, and to start with, I was very unhappy about his arrival and his proposal...or should I say *insistence* that I marry him, but now that we are together, I find him to be a kind, confident, intelligent man who makes me feel safe and loved, so I am thankful to God and our Lord Jesus Christ that he came upon our shores and chose me."

Ravn was quite for a moment as a pang of jealousy hit him. It wasn't that he wanted Kenna. She was beautiful, it was true, but he wanted someone to speak of him that way.

Siggy used to compliment him on being strong and powerful and brave and he'd thought they'd been the only compliments he'd ever need, but to see the softness wash over Kenna's face as she spoke of Haakon, he realized he wanted that too.

But could he hope to find it?

How could they be so different? He and his brother? Was it because he had always followed the darkness, as the runestones had reported? Had his brother followed a path of light and that was why he had a crown, a wife, and likely heirs on the horizon and had swapped one home for another so easily?

Haakon also had people who respected him.

"Here." Kenna handed him a plate of eggs and a spoon. She'd sprinkled salt crystals over it and added a knob of bread.

"Thank you." He took it. "Where do Astrid and Orm sleep?"

"They have taken two empty dwellings on the east."

"One each."

"Aye, my brother, Hamish, has been staying with Astrid each night." Her lips pursed and she shook her head slightly.

"And this bothers you?" He spooned eggs into his mouth. They were good.

"They are not wed."

Ravn laughed. "Astrid is not the marrying sort."

"Which makes her, in my eyes and the eyes of the Lord, a sinner."

"'A sinner'? Why?"

"To lie with a man, she should be married to him."

"And your brother? He is also sinning?"

"Absolutely!" She pointed at the door. "Until she arrived, he'd been celibate, the same as me—"

"What is that?"

"Celibate?"

"Ja."

"It means not to lie with someone. No sex…ever."

"Ah, I see." He paused. "But why would you want no sex ever?"

"It is not forever, but God's will that a union should be blessed before sharing a bed." She paused. "It is the sanctity of marriage they are disrespecting."

He saw the irritation washing over her face. But there was one thing he couldn't quite believe. "Are you telling me that until my sister arrived here, your brother, Hamish, was a virgin?"

"Aye, that is exactly what I'm saying."

He laughed, loudly, and several sleeping Vikings stirred. "Oh, in the name of Thor, she will have thoroughly corrupted him."

"Whatever do you mean?"

"I do not believe there is even a word for celibacy in my language. Sex is free and easy; pleasure is there for the taking. But you know that, right? You are married to my brother."

"What I do in the bedchamber with my husband is none of your business." She held his eye contact with more than a hint of fierceness.

He held up his hand. "I do not wish to offend, Your Grace."

She inclined her head and started eating her own plate of eggs.

"But in our land, when the nights are long and dark and cold," he said, "it is known for many people to take to the same bed. Arms and legs entwine, bodies become one and slick with sweat. Gasps and cries of ecstasy. It is a way to pass the time, a way to keep warm."

Her lips formed a perfect 'o' and her spoon had stopped halfway to her mouth.

"Men with men, women with women, there is no jealousy, no judgment, so you see why I say my sister will have corrupted your virgin brother."

She frowned. "So you would not care if someone took your wife?"

He paused. "Sadly, that is not an issue now that I no longer have a wife."

She made a little cross sign on her chest. "Lord bless her soul."

"She is with the gods," he said quickly. "But I would not have minded her being with another man, as long as it was my idea and I got to watch."

"'Watch'?"

"It would be fun so see her pleasured and know it was my turn next."

"Oh, you really are a heathen." She stood with her plate of food.

"You do not think Haakon would do the same?"

"I have seen him jealous of my childhood friend who looks at me too much or fills up my ale too often, so no, I really don't think he would want another man bedding me." She picked up her drink. "I will finish my food in my room. I wish to check on my owl."

He nodded and suppressed a grin. He'd taught her something new about his people. Something Haakon hadn't bothered to tell her. Was that because Haakon didn't want her asking questions about the orgies he'd enjoyed so recently at Uppsalla? Well, Ravn could guarantee the queen would want answers now. She was clearly not a woman who shared her body with just anyone, so how could she understand a man who would?

Good luck, Haakon.

After finishing his eggs, he stood and threw his cloak over his shoulders. He stepped outside and squinted in the bright light glinting off the snow-covered ground. The fort walls were high and strong and in the distance, he could see the manned watchtower. A well stood to his right, and beyond that, a pigpen and more round dwellings with turf roofs.

It was busy, with villagers moving around, collecting water, tending animals. An ironsmith was at work under a shelter, his furnace flaming and his hammer toiling.

After relieving himself, Ravn made his way east of the Great House and soon saw two small dwellings side by side. Each had the door closed. A black-and-white dog sat outside one chewing lazily on a bone.

He decided to knock on the other door first. If it was Orm, he wouldn't care about knocking, but Astrid would shred his ears if he just walked in on her.

Knock. Knock.

The door flew open with gusto. "Brother!" Orm stood there, his face freshly washed and shaven for once and a big grin balling his clean cheeks. His torso was bare and his pants hung low on his lean hips. "How are you this fine morn?"

Ravn scowled. "Why are you so cheerful?" He hoped it wasn't because he was screwing his pretty thrall. She was a princess. She deserved better treatment.

Unless of course she liked Orm. Ravn shook his head to rid himself of the thought.

"I am cheerful because we are all together." Orm clapped his hand on Ravn's shoulder and pulled him inside. "Please, I bid you to enter my humble abode."

It was compact and round with a central fire and had two fur-covered cots opposite each other. A wonky, wooden table held food and drink and the walls were covered in drying herbs and little animal bones tied on string like decorations.

A bowl of water was set on a stand and had a razor and soap beside it. More water heated over the fire.

Ravn peered into the shadows.

Curled up in the corner was the thrall woman. Her eyes were wide and her fingertips taut on a blanket she was gripping.

"You, get this water changed," Orm said, clicking his fingers.

She jumped up, then steadied herself on the wall when she appeared to unbalance.

Ravn looked at the base of her muddied, emerald-green gown and remembered the chain linking her ankles.

With obvious difficulty, she shuffled to the dirty water bowl and picked it up. She moved to the door.

Ravn reached for it and held it open. "Let me."

She glanced at him with big, scared eyes and squeezed past him to fling the water outside.

For the first time in his life, Ravn wished he weren't so big and intimidating or his voice so gruff. It was clear she was terrified of him and waiting for him to hurt her.

Which he had no intention of doing.

She bustled back in and set about refilling the bowl with warm water from over the fire.

Orm sat on a small chair with a sigh. He held up his dirty, bare feet. "Wash these, thrall. And make sure you get between every toe." He wriggled them. "And if you don't, you'll be trimming my toenails with your teeth."

"Orm." Ravn frowned and sat on another chair. "Why do you have to be like that? She is a princess."

"*Ja*, my princess thrall."

"What is your name?" Ravn asked her.

She didn't answer. Instead, she knelt before Orm and lathered her hands with soap.

"Speak to me," Ravn said, studying the small cross that hung from her earring. "What is your name?"

"Princess Carmel, daughter of King Athol of the Westlands and daughter of Queen Elspeth the Pious."

"Princess Carmel," he repeated, leaning forward. "And where is this Westland?"

"West of here." She held his gaze for a second and a twitch caught her nostril.

She thought him foolish.

He laughed. "I suppose that makes sense."

She didn't answer and set to her task washing his brother's feet.

Ravn turned his head away, not wanting to see her small, dainty fingers on Orm's big, hairy toes.

The door flung open again, a draft coming with it. "I bid you good morn. May the Lord be with us all on this fine day."

A village woman with long, brown hair stood there, cheeks nipped pink by the cold. Her gown was clean and dark blue and she had a cross hanging from her neck. When she spotted Ravn, she stilled.

"Anna!" Orm held up his hands as if in greeting. "You have come to see me. I am so pleased."

"You are?" She tore her attention from Ravn and set a freshly baked loaf on the table.

"*Ja*, because I have a question."

She walked up to Carmel and gently touched her shoulder as if in greeting, then sat beside Orm. Her attention went to him. "Ask away."

"I have seen a bird, a small one with a red chest." He rubbed his chest and frowned. "I have never seen it before, and I wonder, was it injured and bleeding or are its feathers that color always?"

"Ah, it is a robin. A cheerful, little bird, always singing, quite brave."

"*Ja, ja*, he was singing right next to me." Orm beamed. "I am pleased he is not injured."

"You do not get robins in the northlands?" Anna asked.

"No." Orm looked at Ravn. "Have you ever seen such a thing?"

"No." Ravn shook his head and watched as Carmel moved the water aside and then struggled to reach a towel with her legs bound. He shifted to help her.

She took the towel without comment and set to drying his brother's feet.

"You need to take her ankle chains off." Ravn gestured to them.

"What? Why?"

"How can she serve you with them on?" He gritted his teeth, wanting to say more.

"So far, so good." Orm shrugged and reached for the scarf Anna had around her neck. He studied the pattern.

"You need to take them off," Ravn said, a bit firmer.

Orm scowled at him.

"The fort walls are high, the entrance is secure, and even if she did get out, the cold would kill her or the wolves would." He nodded at Carmel. "You know that, right?"

She nodded, just a little.

"I want to know she is with me," Orm said with a scowl.

"Why?" Ravn tipped his head, studying his brother. They'd had a thrall growing up, Joseph, and Orm had never showed any interest in him after his initial curiosity.

"Because she is a princess."

"Ah." Ravn pointed at him. "My point exactly."

"What do you mean?"

"A princess has a brain. She is clever—she knows that there is no point trying to escape. It would be a death wish for certain." He touched her slender shoulder and the delicateness of her flesh and bones shot an arrow of protectiveness through him. "I am right, huh?"

She nodded. "Aye, I would not try to escape. I would not survive."

He smiled. "See, take the chains off, Orm. She will be much more efficient in all the jobs you need her to do."

Orm chewed on his bottom lip. He looked at Anna.

"Aye, take the hog tie off. She is not a horse." Anna nudged him with her elbow.

"You think I should?" he asked her.

Anna glanced at Carmel.

Ravn again sensed a tenuous friendship, or at least respect between the two women.

"I think you should," Anna said. "I think it would show you have compassion in your heart, a very fine quality." She pressed her hand over her breast.

"Mmm." Orm looked from her to Ravn and then to Carmel. "I suppose…"

"I suppose it is up to you. You are her master." Ravn sat back and folded his arms. He didn't like the words that had come from his lips, but he knew Orm would like them and it was a means to an end.

"Oh, do it." He flung up his arms. "The shuffling is annoying me, anyway." He dug into his pocket and found a key. Then he flung it to the floor beside Carmel and it buried itself in the straw.

Quickly, she found it and held it up.

"Here." Ravn took it. "Let me."

Her eyes were wide as he sank to his knees and pushed at the hem of her skirt. Within a few seconds, he'd released the locks on her ankles and removed the heavy iron cuffs.

"Thank you," she said quietly.

"A princess should not be hog-tied," Ravn said, looking up into her green eyes. "But you must promise not to run away. That would make me look a fool for saying you wouldn't."

"I won't." Her bottom lips trembled slightly. "I know I would not make the journey home alone."

He studied the slant of her nose and the tilt of her chin. Her mother, the Queen of the Westlands, would want her back. Men would be searching, an army on the way. Likely, there'd be a hefty reward for her safe return. A beautiful, important woman like this couldn't just be held captive without repercussions.

"We should go and collect eggs," Orm said suddenly jumping up. "Anna, come with me."

"I have not been to my coop yet," she said, standing and smoothing down her gown. "We should be in luck."

Orm shoved his feet into his boots, without his socks, then tore of a hunk off bread. He bit into it and grinned as he chewed. "Stay here, thrall, and tidy my home." He flicked his hand at the bed, spreading crumbs. "Make sure that is clean for me later when I am tired."

She nodded and clasped her hands on her lap. She was still kneeling.

Anna and Orm slipped out, the sealskin that covered the wooden door falling into place and keeping out both the draft and any harsh light.

"Tell me," Ravn said, his voice tense, though he tried not to let it sound that way. "Did my brother touch you last night?"

Chapter Six

CARMEL LOOKED UP at the huge, bearded Viking, hardly believing her ears. "I beg your pardon?"

"Did he fuck you? My brother?"

"What?" She shook her head. "No, thank the Lord above, he didn't." She crossed herself out of habit.

"He didn't touch you at all?"

"No."

"Good." He reached for her upper arms, wrapping his big fingers around them, and then pulled her to standing. "Because that would be wrong. It wouldn't be wrong with just any slave—that would be up to him—but you being a princess, it wouldn't be right, not at all."

His vehemence surprised her. "I didn't think Norsemen had any morals, princess or not." She tilted her right eyebrow. "Or am I mistaken?"

"I think you have heard sagas and I think maybe you have not met the men of Drangar."

"I can safely say I have, as have most of my father's army, much to their peril."

He nodded slowly, still studying her.

His quiet, intense gaze unnerved her as much as Orm's flapping and rapid dialect that seemed to slip into his native tongue, creating a hybrid language that he entertained himself with. She took a step away. "What is wrong with your brother?"

He huffed. "Which one?"

"This one." She gestured to the fur Orm had been sitting on; it was still flattened from his ass.

Ravn chuckled. "He was sent by the gods to test the patience of my parents, and now he tests the patience of his siblings."

"He is…" She hesitated, not wanting to offend the tall bulk of muscle standing before her. "He is excitable."

"*Ja*, he is." He reached forward and crooked his finger beneath her chin, tilting her face to his.

The gentle action had her breath catching in her throat and she tried not to think of the axe, sword, and dagger hanging from his belt or the scar over his right eye that sliced his eyebrow in two.

"He is excitable, but I do not wish him to be excitable with you."

She swallowed, her throat tight.

"What I'm saying is if he tries to take you, mount you, you must shout for me." His lips pressed into a tight line and he shook his head. "I will not have your honor disrespected, not when one day the goddess Freya will question me about my actions here in Tillicoulty."

Carmel wanted to thank Ravn, but what if he said this because he wanted her for himself? What if it was because he wanted to claim her and take her maidenhood?

"So you promise?" he asked. "You will shout for me. I will listen for you, and if you need me, I will be at your side."

"Why?"

He half-smiled. "Why not?"

Suddenly, he stepped away, to the door.

"I don't understand," she said, pulling in a deep breath. "Why are you being like this? I am an enemy of Tillicoulty, and right now, the lowest of the low in this village. Why are you being nice to me?"

He turned slowly to face her, shadows licking over his face. "I have come to learn my place, the way you have yours."

"You are a king and a free man." She held in a huff. "I don't see *your* problem."

"I have also come to see the faces of my constant companions." He paused and held up his hand with three fingers pointing upward. "Regret. Grief. Loneliness. They do not make great bedfellows."

"Grief, I have made friends with." She held back the catch in her voice and blinked a few times to abate the prickle in her lower lids. "My father's head is on a pike just yonder."

He frowned. "For that, I am sorry and I had no part in it."

She turned away to face the wall and stared at a small, black bug climbing up the stonework.

"War is unkind to all who know it."

He was suddenly behind her again, close. His body heat radiated onto her back and his breaths breezed on her neck.

"My mother will be distraught when she hears the news," Carmel whispered. "She loved him very much."

"And she will want vengeance?"

Carmel turned to him, a sudden spark lighting her belly. "Aye, she will. My mother is not a woman to be crossed."

"I sense it runs in the family." He swiped his tongue over his bottom lip, leaving a soft sheen there. "Would your husband agree with me?"

"I am unwed." She held up her left hand. "Look."

"I do not know what that means." He frowned at her fingers.

"No wedding ring." She tutted. This man really was a heathen.

"So does that mean…" He bent his head closer. So close, his nose nearly touched hers and she could see the star inked onto his face in stark detail. Her instincts told her to step back, get away from this brute of a man, but the warrior in her stood her ground and she stared up at him defiantly. "Does that mean what?"

"That you are a virgin?" He raised his eyebrows as though amused at the very thought.

"If you are asking if I am a good Christian girl saving myself for marriage, then aye, I am." A prickle of heat went up her spine and over her scalp. Her breasts tingled and she pressed her legs together as heat went through her. This was not a proper conversation to be having with a man.

"'Girl'? I'd say you were all woman," he murmured, his voice low and dark. "And being the age you are and not knowing what it is like to have a man in your bed, a cock in your cunny, is surely a… What do you call it…? A sin."

A sudden burst of temper gripped her and she placed her hands on his chest and shoved. "How dare you speak of me that way? Of my… Of my…"

He laughed and stepped away. "How dare I talk of your royal cunny? Is that what you mean?"

"Aye." She slammed her hands onto her hips.

"You didn't mind a few moments ago when I said I would protect your cunny's honor from my brother's desires."

Her belly clenched and she swallowed the taste of bile, sickened at the thought of Orm scrabbling between her legs and penetrating her.

"And I will protect you from him," Ravn said, heading to the door again. "But not because I want you, just so we're clear. But from one royal to another, it is the least I can do."

"You are trying to make amends?"

"I'm trying a new path."

"That may be, but it's too late for your soul to be saved. For any of your souls to be saved." She flicked her hand in the direction of the battlefield. "The blood and guts out there tell the story."

"From what I've heard, Tillicoulty did not go searching for this fight, it came to them. Think about that, Princess." He tapped the side of his head. "Think about that."

Suddenly, he was gone, slipping out of the dwelling nimbly for a man of his size.

"Damn you to hell and the devil's eternal flame," she muttered, sloshing ale into a mug. As she sipped, she looked at the chain discarded on the floor. "God giveth, then God taketh away."

What on earth was she going to do about her predicament?

"THRALL!"

Carmel jumped at the sound of Orm's voice hollering from outside. She'd been praying beside her meager bed and enjoying the quiet, calming ritual.

"We need logs." He pushed into the dwelling holding a dead chicken. "Go chop some."

She scrabbled to her feet. "Aye, I'll do it now."

Slipping past him, she felt glad that it was a task that didn't involve her doing something for him directly—washing his feet, plaiting his hair, or pouring his ale.

Outside, the snow still lay on the ground, though it was defrosting in the midday sun and dripped from the turf roofs. She spotted a pile of thick logs beside a tree stump that had an axe lodged into it.

She glanced around. The village was going about its business. Children played, a few older women chatted by the well, a dog chased a cat, and smoke drifted into the sky spreading the pleasant scent of food cooking.

But the scene didn't bring solace to Carmel. This wasn't her home and she wanted to get away. Her castle on the western coast awaited her. A place where good Christians followed the rules of God and the scriptures. A place where she gave the orders and was waited on while her parents deliberated over possible marriage matches—something they could never agree on.

"Lord, give me strength," she muttered as she gripped the axe in the wood. She pulled, then pulled harder—it was lodged solid. Setting her foot on the stump and heaving with all her might, she felt it finally come free, though the force of it had her staggering backward and almost falling over, the axe was so heavy.

With a frown, she reached for a log and balanced it on the stump. The ground was slippery and she secured her footing before raising the hefty axe above her head.

For a moment, it teetered there, almost threatening to tip her over backward with the weight, then she brought it down with a violent blow, slicing the log in half and sending it skittering.

A sense of satisfaction went through her and she reached for another log.

She swung again, but this time, her aim wasn't as accurate and she splintered the side of the log and buried the axe deep into the stump.

"Oh, in the name of…" She gripped it and pulled, trying to free it from its bind. Closing her eyes, she grimaced, then pulled some more. "Damn it." The thing was well and truly stuck.

She glanced at the doorway, wondering if she should ask Orm to get it out.

No. She'd rather he stay away from her.

Another pull and a yank with a twist this time. But it was no good. The blade was lodged in tightly.

"You in a fix?"

She looked up.

Ravn was striding toward her.

"No." She scowled and pulled again.

He stopped with his hands on his hips. He'd removed his cloak and wore a gray tunic with a deep open 'v' at the front that showed chest hair. "You sure?"

"Aye."

She set her foot on the stump to put her entire weight behind her next heave.

He watched her struggle, one eyebrow raised.

"Damn and blast," she muttered, releasing a fast exhalation and stepping away.

"Here. Let me." He curled his fist around the axe handle, gave one effortless yank, and freed it.

Her irritation increased. Sometimes, it was maddening to be a feeble woman.

"Pass me that." He nodded at a log.

"What?"

"Just do it."

She gave him a thick log.

He set it on the stump. "Orm tell you to do this?"

"Aye." She folded her arms.

He brought the axe down with deadly accuracy, splitting the thick log in two with a thwack and sending both pieces falling to the floor. "Next."

"But…"

"Pass me another." He held out his hand.

"Orm will…"

"Orm will what?"

"He told *me* to do this." Despite her protest, she handed over another log.

"And I'll do it for you." He split the log. "Because otherwise, you're going to take your own leg off and then you'll be no use to him or anyone else."

"I can chop logs."

"I'm sure you can, and you could today if you had a lighter axe." He picked up the log she'd splintered but not split and chopped it in two. "This is an axe made for a man. You could do it if you had a woman's axe. Like the one Astrid has."

"Your sister?"

"*Ja.*" He nodded at the log pile. "Keep 'em coming."

She positioned another log on the stump then stepped back as he chopped it. His breath huffed out in front of him and the tendons on his neck strained as he hoisted the heavy axe above his head.

"Hot work," he said after a few minutes and several more logs. He wiped the back of his hand over his glistening brow and chuckled. "Not that I'm complaining. Back in Drangar, it's hard to get hot this time of year."

"How many people live in Drangar?"

"A few hundred, not including the children."

"And it is by a river?"

He hit another log, splitting it into two perfectly equal halves. "It is on the shore of a fjord."

"What is a fjord?"

"An inlet of water, with mountains either side." He set down the axe and gripped the base of his tunic. In one swift movement, he pulled it up over his head and tossed it to the side, where it landed on a stack of the split logs.

Carmel swallowed, her throat suddenly tight. It wasn't that she hadn't seen a man's naked torso before—of course she had—but never one like Ravn's. His muscles had muscles and his belly was a series of bricks. His pectorals were wide and defined and the round balls of his shoulders led to thick, bulging biceps; the right had a long scar. A strip of dark hair ran from his navel to his pants and his left nipple was pierced with a silver bar.

He narrowed his eyes at her. "What?"

She tore her attention away and grabbed another log to be split. "Here."

In one smooth movement, he drew the axe over his head then crashed it down. Tendons flexed beneath his smooth, golden flesh and he grunted with the effort.

"Brother, what are you doing?" Orm appeared with his hands in the air. "That is the job of my thrall."

"This axe is too heavy for her." Ravn held the handle in both hands and tossed it upward before catching it. "You should be more thoughtful."

"Huh, why do I need to be when you are here?" He tapped the side of his head. "Though it is not a trait I remember in you. Oh, no, you usually only think of yourself."

Ravn huffed and indicated for another log.

Carmel was quick to provide it.

"And on the subject of you being here, when are you leaving?" Orm asked, skipping backward as the split log flew his way and crashed to the ground at his feet.

"Why? You don't like my company?"

"There is a reason I left Drangar." Orm shrugged.

"You left because of father as much as me."

"That might be true." Orm twiddled his thumbs in a fast, frantic movement. "But now you have taken his place as king."

"So you would have stayed if Haakon had killed me and he'd become King of Drangar?"

Carmel watched as Orm rolled his eyes and twisted his mouth as though thinking intensely. The brothers had a very strange relationship and a history she didn't understand.

"Er, maybe I would have and maybe I wouldn't." Orm shrugged. "You'll never know."

Ravn huffed and reached for another log. He balanced it then brought down the axe. A sheen of sweat sat between his shoulder blades and on the hair at his sternum.

"I will leave you," Orm said. "You seem to enjoy the company of my thrall." He cackled and said something in his native language then threw his hand in the air and turned.

"Fool," Ravn muttered.

Carmel folded her arms, hugging herself, if Ravn had taken her as his thrall, life maybe wouldn't have been so bad.

No! What was she thinking? She didn't want to be a slave to either of the heathen brothers.

Chapter Seven

THE DAYS TURNED into weeks and then a month went by. The frost and snow melted and small, yellow flowers sprung up wherever there was space. Geese flew overhead, honking as they moved from one home to another. The sun woke earlier and set later, spreading long shadows on the growing crops.

Carmel was still a prisoner in Tillicoulty. She was a slave to Orm's constant needs and her prayers remained unanswered.

"Carmel," Anna said, rushing over to where Carmel sat weaving a basket with Fion—one of the older ladies in the village who seemed to have taken a shine to Carmel. "A meeting is being called in the Great House."

"Today?" Fion asked, looking up and patting her graying bun as though checking for stray strands.

"Aye, and King Haakon says Carmel must attend."

"Oh." Carmel looked between the two women. "But...why me?" She was the lowest of the low—Orm told her that often enough. She had no voice in the village she'd sought to attack so viciously alongside her father.

"Come on." Anna plucked the basket from Carmel's hand and pulled her up. "They are waiting."

"Who is waiting?" Carmel asked.

"Them. All of them...the Vikings."

Carmel hoisted her pants up her lean hips—a gift from Anna when her gown had become unwearable—and straightened her tunic. She tucked her hair behind her ears—it was loose today, as she'd just washed it with a jug of warm water and rosemary soap and was waiting for it to dry completely.

"But why must I be there?"

"Because the meeting is about *you*." Anna linked her hand through Carmel's arm as they walked.

"Me?"

"Aye, you are a big problem, don't you know?"

"How can I be a big problem?" Carmel shook her head. "I have done nothing other than obey Orm's every command and speak only when spoken to."

"You are a problem because you are a princess, and not a princess of Tillicoulty."

"That is true." Carmel saw that the doorway to the Great House had been propped open now that the weather was more temperate. "I am a princess and I am no doubt being missed."

"And likely a rescue mission is being planned as we speak."

Carmel said nothing. Much as she liked Anna and some of the other villagers, she knew they were on borrowed time. Her mother would be convening an army, assembling the best men and the most skilled warriors. And likely now that the weather was better, they'd soon be making an appearance. Heck, if God was being merciful, they'd be camped by the river right now and just picking their moment.

Aye, surely that was where they were. Right now.

Her stomach roiled with excitement at the thought of being rescued and going home, but she didn't show her anticipation. Instead, she ducked into the Great House and let her eyes adjust to the dimness.

She spotted King Haakon first, seated upon his tall-backed chair with Queen Kenna at his side. Lined beside benches laden with ale jugs and bread were some of the men of the village, Noah, Olaf, Bryce, and Hamish, plus several others she hadn't deigned to speak to. Opposite them were Astrid—busy whittling arrowheads—Orm, and Ravn.

Her attention stayed on Ravn.

Why?

Because as it so often was, his attention was settled on her. Intense. Unwavering. Absolute. It was as if he were trying to see right into her and figure her out. See her deepest, darkest thoughts and the bare bones of her soul.

"Ah, good, you are here," King Haakon said. "We await your counsel, Princess Carmel."

"My… My counsel?" she managed, twisting her hands in front of herself. It was rare for anyone to address her by title here in Tillicoulty, let alone the king.

"*Ja*, we wish to know what is to come from your people," Haakon said, holding his mug out for ale.

A villager filled it.

"I have told you." Astrid stopped what she was doing and looked up at her brother. "The runes bring a forecast of invasion and bloodshed. Berkana heeds preparation."

Carmel forced herself to stop fidgeting and tilted her chin. "Who is Berkana?"

Astrid frowned her way. "The Birch Goddess. The stone also advises caution if you find yourself in an unfortunate domestic situation, which is apparently what has happened to you, thrall."

Carmel didn't answer, but she held Astrid's challenging glare for a few seconds before turning back to Haakon. "How would I know what is to come when I am here?"

"You know your people," Haakon said.

"I know my mother is a queen of great power and determination."

"And she loves you?" Kenna asked.

"Aye, she does."

"So she will search for you." Kenna took Haakon's hand. "We would search the world twice over if a daughter of ours went missing."

"That is true." He kissed the backs of his wife's knuckles. "And may we be blessed with daughters as well as sons one day."

Kenna smiled and rubbed her belly.

"Spring has arrived," Noah said, tugging at his beard. "We should expect an invasion any day."

"I prefer to think of it as an opportunity to negotiate," King Haakon said. "To discuss how we will charge King Athol's heirs when they use our land in the future."

"My father's heir is my brother, Seamus. He is only eleven and he is king now. It is him you must negotiate with."

Haakon nodded slowly.

"And he is not yet a warrior." The thought of something happening to sweet, young Alfred didn't bear thinking about. "I doubt he will be with any traveling army."

"And your mother?"

"She may well journey. She is fit and strong."

"Like her daughter," Ravn said. "Good stock."

"We are not a pen of pigs about to be bartered." She narrowed her gaze at Ravn. "So do not compare us as such."

He threw back his head and laughed. "No, no, you are not a sow from a pen of pigs. I can attest to that."

Astrid half-smiled and her eyebrows twitched. "She does not tolerate your drollness, King Ravn."

"Another fine quality." He tugged on his beard and smiled at Carmel. "That I have only just become appreciative of."

"We should journey to the falls to see if they are in the valley yet," Hamish said. "I am happy to volunteer."

"And I will go with him," the huge Viking Gunner said. "We will return swiftly if we take rested horses."

"*Ja*, that is a good idea." Haakon nodded at the door. "Go now, but be sure not to be seen.

Hamish stood, stepped over to Astrid, and set a kiss on the top of her head. She didn't acknowledge him, just carried on working at her arrowhead. Though Carmel did see the briefest hint of a smile tugging at her lips.

"God's speed," Noah said, crossing himself. The man at his side with the long, gray beard did the same.

The two tall men left the Great House.

"I have a question," Orm said, flapping his arm in the air.

"Go on." Haakon nodded at him.

"When is Ravn returning to Drangar? This is a busy village with two kings."

"You are so keen to get rid of me," Ravn said, sitting back and folding his arms. "Why is that?"

"I do not like your face." Orm circled his own and pouted.

Ravn turned to Haakon. "Now that the weather has changed and the sea is calm, I will return to Drangar as soon as I get the boat stocked." He nodded at the handful of crew who had traveled with him. "The men are keen to get back to their families and work their land. Also, I have my people awaiting me, their leader. There is much to do for a town that size to prosper."

"*Ja*," Haakon said with a nod. "And you can take news of us to the people of Drangar."

"I will." Ravn pressed his hand to his chest. "They will be pleased to hear of your good fortune."

Haakon leaned forward. "And you, brother? Are you pleased for our good fortune?"

"*Ja*, of course."

"You would not have been at one time." Astrid stared at Ravn.

"I am a changed man." He paused. "Loss can do that to a person."

Orm laughed. "You can change no more than an apple can change to a turnip."

"Then you do not know my heart." Ravn picked up a drink and took a slug.

"Your black heart," Astrid said.

"Black, maybe, but also broken. Losing a wife, child, and father all within a few weeks does that to a man."

Quietness descended. A few people looked at one another.

"And now my son, Thormod, awaits me." Ravn stood. "And he will need a new mother, so I will take her." He pointed straight at Carmel. "A mother with royal blood, if not Viking blood, will do nicely."

"What?" Carmel's mouth hung open as she stared at Ravn. "I will not go with you."

"It was not a question, but a statement." Ravn shrugged.

Her vision of returning to her castle, her mother and brother, and with views of the sunset over the sea shrank from her grasp. "No. I refuse." She turned to Haakon. "Please, Your Grace, I beg you."

Haakon frowned. "Why would I let you take our hostage, Ravn?"

"*Ja*, you cannot take her. She is mine." Orm jumped up.

Ravn ignored him. "It makes perfect sense," he said. "When the army comes for her, you can say she was taken by invading forces to a land faraway. It will prevent a battle, avoid the spilling of more Tillicoulty blood, and it is the truth."

Haakon looked at Kenna, who gave a small nod.

"What! No!" Carmel rushed up to Haakon. "It's a crazy idea. I can't leave these shores. This land is my home."

"You don't get a say in it," Haakon said. "You attacked our people and now you are our prisoner."

"Aye, *your* prisoner, not his." She pointed at Ravn. "He wasn't even here when I arrived."

"She is my prisoner, my thrall. I captured her." Orm slammed his hand into his fist. "I will not let you take her, brother. I will chain her to…to…to me." He glanced around as though looking for the ankle chains.

"But it is a solution," Noah said. "We get to save face because we have not handed a hostage over, yet there is no need for a battle. What would they gain by attacking if she is not here?"

Ravn nodded slowly and crossed his arms. He gave Carmel a look of smug satisfaction and ignored Orm, who ran past him and out of the meeting.

"No!" Carmel said, marching up to Ravn. "I will not go with you. I will not be a mother to your motherless son. He is not mine. I did not birth him. I will not do it. I will not leave my beloved homeland." She pressed her hands together and looked upward. "Dear Lord Almighty, please be with me in this time of need."

"He will not help you and you will leave with me," Ravn said.

Ravn was so sure and calm, it made her blood boil. "You are a selfish boar-head and no wonder loneliness is your best friend." She jabbed his hard chest. "You think only of yourself."

He scowled at her. "That is not true, I—"

She turned and stomped past Noah and Anna, going out the door into the bright daylight. She didn't want to hear Ravn's deep, accented voice full of excuses for his barbaric behavior.

The first thing her eyeline settled on was the watchtower and she made straight for it. She'd go. Run away. Take her chances. There was a very strong likelihood her mother's army was at the valley campsite right now. She only had to reach there and then tell them to retreat with her in tow.

Or maybe attack but with advance warning of the Norsemen's hideous tactics.

"Carmel!" Anna called. "Wait."

Carmel ignored her and pushed into a sprint. She wasn't hanging around to be stowed onto a longboat and taken to foreign shores against her will.

"Hey, stop!" Anna called again, her voice a little closer.

Carmel sped up, her hair whipping behind her and her breaths quickening.

"You there. Halt!" a villager on the watchtower shouted down at her. "I order you to halt in the name of King Haakon."

Again, she ignored the instruction to stop and flew out of the village. She took the track between the neat rows of crops that led east, toward the forest. The dark shadows of the trees were welcoming; they'd embrace her, hide her.

On and on she raced, thankful for the fact that she'd always been a good runner. She tore past rows of beans on poles, sprouting cabbages, and spring greens. Making it past a couple of horses grazing, Carmel found new hope springing inside of her.

She was gaining on the forest. Anna wasn't calling her any-more. She'd done it. She'd gotten away from the devilish Vikings who sought to own her.

"Carmel." A deep, breathless voice.

Her heart roiled and her stomach clenched. A gasp caught in her throat. Taking a moment to look over her shoulder, she saw Ravn racing up behind her with a look of such fierce determina-tion, she knew her chances of escape had just been drastically reduced.

"Stay away from me!" she shouted, taking a sharp left and choosing a different route into the forest. She felt like a deer being hunted and trying to outmaneuver teeth and claws and arrows and spears.

Panic twisted her guts and a new speed gave her legs energy.

But then he was behind her. His heavy breaths and the stomp of his feet on the earth thudding in her ears.

"No!" she wailed as his arm came around her waist, pulling her to his hard body.

Then she was flying through the air, a moment of suspension. She braced, waiting for impact.

It came, but not as hard as expected because she landed on top of Ravn, her body sprawled over his. Her hair filled her face and her legs were akimbo.

He grunted on his collision with the earth then wrapped his other arm around her, holding her close as though not trusting her not to jump up and run away again.

"Get off me!" She wriggled and shoved at him.

"In the name of Odin… woman… would you just stop?" He was breathless and his arms like vises around her.

She could feel the entire length of his body against hers. "How dare you? God sees this and His wrath will rain down."

"You will feel my wrath in a minute and—"

She jabbed her knee into his groin.

His sudden long groan was deep and guttural. For a moment, his grip on her slackened as his face twisted in agony.

Making the most of it, she pushed to the right, rolling off him.

But she didn't get far because suddenly, he was over her, pinning her to the ground, her arms either side of her head and his weight as binding as any ball and chain.

"You brutish monster," she hissed up at him. "How dare you?"

"I dare." Furrowed lines plowed over his brow. "Because you are a brat, my little princess. You are a brat."

She squirmed, thrusting her hips and legs. It was no use. She couldn't shake him off. "Do not speak to me that way." She was breathing hard. "You have no idea who I am."

"And you have no idea who I am." His grip on her tightened and he lowered his face so his nose was bumping up against hers. "You have absolutely no idea what I am capable of, so quit this nonsense."

"Urgh!" She twisted harder, but to no avail.

He sucked in a breath, his eyes flashed, and his grip on her forearms tightened.

She'd never felt so trapped, not even when Orm had carried her from the battlefield and cuffed her ankles.

"Let me go."

"You are coming with me to the northlands."

"I am not."

"You are. Say it."

"No!"

"You are coming with me and you will behave and you will be a mother to my son. Say it."

"Why on God's earth would you want that? Any of it?"

"Because…" He swiped his tongue over his bottom lip. "Because I want you."

She stilled. Frozen. "You told me you didn't. That you wouldn't." Heat filled her pussy just at the thought of being naked with him and his cock filling her. It was a sin of the highest order to even think such a thing, but to physically react to it? *Oh, Lord, have mercy.*

Her breath hitched in her chest and her heart skipped a strange beat.

"I didn't say I wanted your gold-plated cunny, Princess. I said I wanted you."

She curled her hands into fists. "You could get anyone to tend your son."

"I don't want anyone."

"And I don't want to leave these shores."

"It is the only way to protect Tillicoulty and the people my siblings have come to care about." He paused and searched her eyes as though looking for something. "I need to atone. I need you to understand that."

"Atone without me. Praise be to the Lord. I am not your salvation, Ravn."

"You are exactly that." He lowered his face.

He filled her vision. His lips were only a hairsbreadth from hers.

"The gods put you in my path for a reason, Carmel."

"What reason?"

"That, I have yet to understand, but until I do, you are coming with me."

Suddenly, he sprang up, nimbly for a man of his size. He stooped and took hold of her arm, hoisting her to standing.

She shoved at him and pushed her hair from her face. Looking down, she brushed the leaves and twigs from her clothing.

"Where did you think you were going?" he asked.

"To my people."

"You don't even know if they are there." He frowned. "Or do you?"

"How could I? I am trapped here!" She pointed at the fort. "But I know my mother and she will not delay now that spring is here. God willing, she is only moments away."

"In which case, we should set sail while the weather is fair."

"What? No." Oh, dear Lord above, had she just hastened her fate?

"It will not take long to restock the boat. My crew has made the few repairs needed and she is ready to sail."

"But… But… Orm. He will not let you take me."

Ravn curled his arm around her waist and urged her back along the track. "Orm does not get a say in it."

"That's not what *he* thinks."

"I am his big brother and a king. He will do as I say."

The determination in Ravn's tone made her believe him.

Chapter Eight

RAVN KEPT A tight hold of his slippery princess. She could run, he'd give her that, and aim a swift one with her knee too. His balls still ached.

He frowned as he stomped ahead, towing her at his side. His plan hadn't been to hit the seas today, but he would. He couldn't trust her not to slip away in the night. He wouldn't get a moment of rest while they were still ashore.

Anna ran up to meet them. Her cheeks were flushed. "Carmel, why would you run? The forest is dangerous and—"

"You would run if you were me," Carmel snapped.

Ravn bit back a smile. It seemed a sharp tongue appealed to him—a woman who said what she thought and didn't layer words in honey so they would be sweet to his ears.

As he'd spent time with Carmel over the last few weeks—always under the pretense of helping her with chores—he'd come to admire her spirit and sense of self. She had a confidence his wife had never had. A way of saying things that made him think anew. Perhaps it was her god that gave her a different perspective. Maybe it was because she was unique.

Coming up with the plan to take her back to Drangar had been a good one. Win-win for him. He'd been away long enough, he was in danger of being usurped by some would-be king— Helga could only hold the fort for so long—and his son needed to know his face. Returning with sagas of his siblings, a new land, and with a regal new woman in tow would do his reputation good. A lot of good.

"And don't try it again!" the watchman shouted down as they walked beneath the tower. He shook his pike. "You can never escape."

"I can if the good Lord has mercy and takes me to heaven," she muttered.

"You will like Drangar," Ravn said softly. "It is like…heaven."

"I think you mean hell."

"I do not know what hell is. But if it's cold and mountainous and full of bears, elk, and wolves, then *ja*, that is what it is like."

She said nothing. Her body was tense as though turned to wooden planks as she walked.

"Where did you go?" Orm rushed up to them, his face flushed and his kohled eyes wide and manic. "You bad thrall."

"Carmel took off," Anna said, "but Ravn brought her back."

"You took off?" Orm stepped up close to her, his mouth a severe, flat line. "You ran away."

"I'd still be running if I had the choice." She glared at him. "My life here with you is miserable and with your brother, it will be torturous. You are an imbecile, Orm, a pathetic creature who barely resembles a man and may God have mercy on your mad soul when you crawl at the gates of heaven and—"

Orm raised his hand, palm flat.

Ravn recognized the fury flashing in his brother's eyes. Orm hated to be told he was mad.

Quickly, Ravn snapped out his hand and caught Orm's wrist seconds before it connected with Carmel's cheek.

She flinched, nestling closer to Ravn as a gasp caught in her throat.

"Don't you ever," Ravn said, anger making his jaw so tense, it was hard to speak, "raise a hand to this woman again."

Orm was breathing hard, spittle in the corner of his mouth.

"Do I make myself clear?" Ravn asked, a brittle ache clawing at his heart at the thought of someone hurting Carmel.

"She is mine. I pulled her from the battlefield. She is mine."

Orm glared harder at Ravn.

"No!" Ravn stepped closer to his brother. "She is mine." He tapped Orm on the side of his head. "Get used to that, as of now, this minute, she is mine."

"No, she is mine."

"No. Mine!"

"*She* is a woman and a princess," Anna said, slamming her hands onto her hips. "And a neat shot with a spear, from what I've heard. She doesn't belong to anyone except herself."

Ravn turned to Anna.

Orm did the same.

"Look at her!" Anna said, gesturing. "She is beautiful, regal, and with a sharp mind too. Stop saying you own her. No one owns her except for our dear Lord above who one day will shepherd her into His flock for all eternity."

"'Flock'?" Orm asked, wrinkling his nose.

"Beautiful," Ravn said, looking down at Carmel, who was still locked in the circle of his arm.

It was true. She was slight of frame but stood tall. She was beautiful because of the way she held herself, the tilt of her chin, the tip of her lips, the curious narrowing of her eyes when she asked him a question and was keen for the answer.

His heart thudded in a way he'd become used to when he saw her for the first time each day. The gods had put her in his way to challenge him, he was sure, but what the challenge was, he couldn't guess.

"I thank you, Anna, my friend," Carmel said, shaking herself loose of Ravn. "And now I have chores."

He let her go. Allowed her to walk back to the dwelling she shared with Orm.

"Pack," he called after her. "We leave on the next tide."

"I have nothing to pack other than my faith in Jesus Christ, our Lord." She held up her hand, her middle finger pointing directly upward in a gesture that could only be described as defiantly disrespectful.

THE LONGBOAT WAS quickly loaded with supplies for the journey north. Ravn's crew of five had made the necessary repairs to the sails and hull and there was nothing left to do except climb aboard.

He walked to the beach with his siblings. The sun shone down and as they navigated through the dunes, orange-and-black butterflies fluttered around the swaying white flowers.

"Njord is kind today," Haakon said, nodding at the ocean.

It was flat and smooth, barely a ripple upon it.

"*Ja*," Ravn said, clasping his brother's shoulder. "It is the gods' way of telling us we must leave Tillicoulty now."

"I don't want him to take my thrall, Haakon," Orm whined as he threw a stone into the air and caught it with a snatch of his hand.

"She is going. It is for the best," Haakon said.

"I found her. I want to keep her," Orm went on.

"Get used to it," Ravn said. "She's coming with me."

"Good riddance," Astrid huffed. "Every time I look at Carmel, I think how close she came to killing Hamish."

Hamish, who walked at Astrid's side, rubbed a fading scar on his brow.

Astrid touched Hamish's cheek. A tender gesture, and one Ravn wasn't ordinarily used to seeing from his sister but had noticed it more and more when she was around Hamish. Tall and broad and hair the same color as hers, Hamish seemed to have a secret way of being with her, one that suited them both and didn't need explaining to anyone. Ravn was happy for her. There'd been no man in Drangar who could tame Astrid and much as it was a surprise that this quiet, pale foreigner had captured her heart, he was glad—he also knew there must have been a lot more beneath the surface when it came to Hamish. Astrid wasn't a woman to settle.

Ravn glanced over his shoulder to make sure Carmel was following through the dunes.

She was walking with Anna and Kenna, a large cloak thrown around her shoulders with the hood drawn up. Her expression was dark, her mouth downturned. For all the world, it looked as though she were heading for the hangman's noose, not a new life.

"You think the people of Drangar will accept her?" Haakon asked.

"*Ja*, I will tell them to."

"She does not speak their language. She does not worship our gods." Haakon took a turn toward the small pier and the waiting longboat.

Ravn kept pace with him. "She is a woman of great resources. Look at how she now walks with the Queen of the Tillicoulty, a place she attacked not so long ago."

"The queen is benevolent." Haakon set his hand over his chest. "She sees the good in everyone."

"A gracious quality," Ravn acknowledged.

"You like her?" Haakon asked. There was a note of tension in his voice, as though Ravn's answer mattered.

Ravn was surprised. "Brother of mine from the womb." He slapped his hand on Haakon's back. "I could not be happier for you that the gods led you to Kenna. She is the beat of your heart—I can see that—and you hers." He paused. "And there is wisdom and kindness in her eyes. She will give you great sons, I am sure of it."

Haakon stopped at the side of the boat. He turned to Ravn and squinted in the sunshine as he studied him. "What has happened to you, brother?"

Ravn laughed. "What do you mean?"

"I mean you never even did that..."

"What?"

"Laugh... You never laughed before."

Ravn straightened his face and sighed. "I have had great loss and with that came time to have a deep think about who I am and what the gods want for me."

"And?"

"And I believe my lust for power had taken me off the path of my destiny. It is why I came to find you." He touched Haakon's arm ring and then his own. "Our father gave us these to remind us of our bond with each other and the gods. For a while, I forgot that. I disrespected it, but that will never happen again." He paused. "If you had not found happiness here, I would have invited you back to Drangar so we could rule together."

"You would not have!"

Ravn tipped his head. "*Ja*, you are right. I would not have gone that far."

Haakon let out a great guffaw. "The gods are wise and I am glad you are following your destiny again."

"I am, brother, I am." He reached out and embraced Haakon in a short, sharp hug. "And 'haps she is my destiny too." He pulled back and nodded at Carmel.

Haakon studied her for a moment and then in their own tongue said, "Her royal blood makes her a good match for you, but do not forget these people have one god who rules their thoughts. You must not disrespect that. If you do, she will hate you forever." He paused. "Their god also insists they are virgins until they marry." He raised his eyebrows at Ravn. "You must be gentle when you take her that first time."

"I know that, brother." Ravn shrugged. "I know all of that, but trust me, I will win her 'round and have her in my bed willingly."

Haakon raised his eyebrows. "Good luck with that. It's not easy, brother. Believe me, I know."

"Any advice, then?"

"Patience. A barrel load of patience."

"Goodbye, brother." Astrid held up her hand.

"Next time I see you, you will have sons, I am sure." Ravn stepped up to Astrid and pulled her into a hug.

She grunted and pushed him away but was smiling. "Get off."

He laughed and clasped Hamish on the shoulder. "Look after my sister, right?"

"She can look after herself, but aye, I'll be at her side." Hamish slipped his arm around Astrid's waist and pulled her close.

"Orm." Ravn looked at Orm.

He was still tossing the stone into the air and catching it. His shoulders were rounded and his sulky mouth downturned. Black kohl streaked down his cheeks to his jawline.

"Orm," Ravn said again. "Be safe."

"Oh, just bloody go," Orm said with a flick of his hand. "And don't come back."

"I will and when I do, you will be a married man." Ravn gestured to Anna. "It is the gods' plan for you, I would wager it."

Orm's mouth fell open as he stared wide-eyed at Anna. The stone rolled to the wooden pier and splashed into the water.

She clasped her hand over her mouth and stepped back, hiding her face.

Ravn laughed and indicated for his crew to board. They did so amidst shouts of goodbye and stomps of boots.

"Princess," Ravn called, "come here. It is time to board."

She folded her arms and glowered at him.

"Now!" He flicked his hand.

"Why would I willingly step aboard a longboat with you?"

"Because I told you to."

"And you are my new master?" Her eyes narrowed and she pouted.

"I am your new king." He pointed at the boat. "Now get on."

"No." She folded her arms.

"You are a disobedient wench." He marched up to her, irritation pricking at him.

"That may be, but I will not board a boat that is to take me away from my homeland against my will." She stuck out her chest and closed her eyes. "I would die first. Stab me here." She banged her right breast dramatically.

"Oh, in the name of Odin, you might be the biggest mistake

of my life." He tutted then stooped and scooped her up into his arms. She was light and delicate and he clasped her to his chest and strode to the plank between pier and boat.

"Hey! Put me down." She yanked his tunic and kicked her legs. "Put me down."

"Goodbye, my brothers. Goodbye, my sister. May the gods always look upon you and the good people of Tillicoulty with great favor."

He boarded the boat in several quick strides, jumping the few feet down to the hull.

Carmel let out a squeal, part shock, part protest.

He kept hold of her, enjoying the warmth of her body against his and the rosemary scent that wafted from her sun-warmed hair.

His crew quickly released the ropes and Haakon and Hamish gave the longboat a shove with their feet setting it adrift.

"Goodbye," Queen Kenna called with a wave. "May God bless you all and Saint Christopher row beside you during your travels." She kissed the cross at her neck.

"Son of Odin and brother of Thor, our great god Meili will be at your side," Orm yelled as he held his arms to the sky. "Meili, be wise and good and protect our brothers from the great serpents and beasts of the ocean."

"Thank you, Orm." Ravn held his hand up. A sudden pang of loss hit him. He'd made amends with his siblings these last weeks. Sure, they still irked him—he'd always have rivalry with Haakon and he'd never understand Astrid—but he could travel home knowing they were happy and healthy.

His father would be pleased as he looked down from Valhalla. If Ravn's penance for his selfish ways had been to lose everyone he'd cared for, he'd now gone some way to compensating for his actions and rebuilding bridges.

"Get off me." Carmel whacked him on the shoulder.

He looked down at her. Her eyes were misted with tears and her bottom lip quivered.

"What is it?"

She blinked and a tear escaped. Quickly, she dashed at it. "Put me down."

He set her feet on the hull but kept his arm around her waist. "Why are you crying?"

"I'm not." She sniffed and turned away from the crowd on the pier.

"I'll take care of you," he said, his voice a little softer as he spoke by her ear. "You're safe with me. I promise."

"Safe with a big brute of a Viking who has dragged me away from my lands?" She gave a dismissive grunt. "I doubt it."

"I am big and strong. I can protect you." He paused. "You had to leave, Carmel. You could not stay in Tillicoulty. Your presence put all of those people in danger." He gestured to the beach as the boat began to move out to sea.

"You could have let me go home."

"You *are* going home, to your new home... Your new home with me."

Chapter Nine

CARMEL SAT BESIDE the central mast huddled in her cloak. She closed her eyes and prayed for deliverance from the awful quandary in which she'd found herself. It seemed she was just lurching from one to another right now.

The Vikings rowed at a steady pace, the constant clunk and splash a rhythm that moved the boat. As they rowed, they sang in a language she didn't understand.

With her eyes closed, she imagined her castle at this time of year. The tiny, blue flowers would be blooming, and the chicken coop full of fluffy, yellow chicks. Out in the field, hares would gamble, leaping into the air and standing up on their back legs to box one another.

Spring was usually her favorite time of year, a season when God truly showed His creative side.

"Here."

She didn't look up at the sound of Ravn's voice.

"You need to drink."

"I'm not thirsty."

"Doesn't matter. If you get dry, you'll feel sicker."

"I don't feel sick."

"Good, now drink." He thrust a mug at her. Several drips sloshed onto her tunic.

With a frown, she brushed the drips away and took the drink. She had a sip. Ale.

"More."

She took several gulps then wiped the back of her hand over her mouth. "Happy now?"

"*Ja.*" He set the mug aside. "Come over here."

"No."

"I want to show you something."

"There is nothing to see except water." She pulled her knees up and hooked her arms around them, staring at her boots.

"There is. The sea is alive."

She pursed her lips. With every second that passed, she was traveling farther from home, farther from her mother, brother, and the memory of her father.

"You can sulk like an annoying little girl or you can make the most of your situation," he said, cupping her chin and forcing her to look up at him. "Which is it to be?" His blue eyes flashed as he stared at her.

"A situation that is not of my choosing." She held his eye contact.

"Which is all part of life's rich path." He paused. "Wouldn't your god want you to be gracious about the path you find yourself upon?"

"What do you know of my God?"

"Very little." He reached for her hands, taking them in his big, warm ones, and pulled her to standing. "But I'm sure he'd want you to see this."

"See what?"

"Come up here." He tugged her toward the front of the boat, stepping over barrels and blankets and past a cage holding clucking chickens. It was hard to walk on a narrow boat that was being swished along by sturdy rowers, even if the sea was mercifully calm.

"Stand here," Ravn said, slotting her next to the neck of the big serpent that decorated the prow. "And hold on."

She did as instructed, looping one arm around the wood, the surface carved to resemble scales.

He stood close behind her, his chest to her back and pointed over her right shoulder. He smelled of ale and leather and chestnut soap. "Out there, look."

"I can't see anything." She shielded her eyes from the glare of the sun. "Only water, which is what I expected."

"No, look." A hint of excitement laced his voice.

She searched the surface. All she could see was the reflection of the sky and the two fluffy, white clouds floating in it. "There is nothing there."

"Wait," he whispered, his breath warm on her temple. "They'll show themselves in a moment."

"What will?" Her heart rate quickened.

He said nothing.

"What is under the water?" Was it a monster? An ugly sea beast? A great, big, ferocious fish that would eat them up with mean jaws and sharp teeth?

"Ravn?" She swallowed tightly as her imagination ramped up. "I'm scared. What is it?"

He slid his thick arm around her waist, holding her to him. "Don't be scared."

She gripped his hard forearm and leaned back against him, glad of his support when her knees felt a little weak.

"Look! There!" He pointed forward. "Can you see?"

The surface had been breached several times, white froth and ripples spreading out in great rings.

"No… I… Oh… What is that?"

A creature had leaped from the water. Gray, sleek, and shiny, it was as long as a person with bright eyes and a mouth shaped almost like a smile. It disappeared as quickly as it had appeared. She knew for sure it wasn't a seal. Not that shape.

"Did you see it?" he asked, squeezing her closer and his body warming hers. "It is beautiful, *ja*?"

"Aye, it is…but…but what is it?" She'd never seen anything like it, not in real life or in a tapestry or piece of artwork.

"A delfin and…there are more…over there."

It was true. There were more delfins. Three, four, five…

They were skimming the surface of the water, their smooth bodies breaching then dipping under. Another leaped out, apparently just for the joy of it. Its intelligent gaze was set on them before hitting the sea again.

"You have seen them before?" she asked.

"*Ja*, many times, but I could never get bored. I could watch them all day."

"I never knew such a thing existed."

"The ocean is a magical place." His mouth was against her as he spoke. "Full of surprises and wonder. You just have to open your eyes to see the gifts it can give you."

"They are a gift from God." She stared in awe as the delfins came closer still, seeming to look up at her as she stood watching them skim through the water.

"Today, they are my gift to you, my beautiful princess."

She turned to look at him. He kept his arm around her, holding her close. "What did you just say?"

"I said they are my gift to you…" He lowered his face. "My beautiful princess."

"That is what I thought you said." She pressed her hands onto his chest. "But why speak that way? I am just a thrall, am I not?"

She saw something new flash in his eyes. Desire. Need. Want. Her breath hitched and for the first time, she realized why he'd brought her on this journey. It wasn't to be his slave, or a mother to his son, and it certainly wasn't to save Tillicoulty. It was because he wanted her to be his woman. Whether that was to be his wife and queen or his whore, she wasn't sure.

"Because you are beautiful," he said. "And beauty deserves beauty."

"You lied."

"About what?" He raised his eyebrows.

"You acted as though you were doing your brother a favor by taking me away, but it suits you, doesn't it?"

"Go on…" His lips twitched as though holding in a smile.

"I'm not just going to be a mother to your son, am I?"

"You can be whatever you want to be." He tucked a strand of her hair behind her ear.

"I want to be a princess to my people, to live in my castle."

"That can't happen. You must accept your new life."

"And if I can't?"

"You will. I'll make damn sure of it. You'll be happy too." He dipped his head and pressed his lips to hers.

His beard tickled. His lips were warm and soft and he tasted slightly salty. Carmel knew she should pull away, push him away, but she stayed frozen in place as he gently kissed her. After a few moments, his tongue peeked between her lips and stroked against hers. Still, she didn't stop him.

But although she was deathly still, her heart raced, her stomach clenched, and a tremble traveled down her spine, taking heat with it to between her legs. This was her first kiss and never in a million years could she have predicted it would be with a wild Viking on his longboat as he stole her away to new lands.

He pulled back and cupped her face with one warm hand. Studied her eyes as if trying to gauge her response to his boldness.

"My mother would have you hanged for that," she managed, then she swiped her tongue over her bottom lip to retrieve his flavor.

"She'd have to catch me first." He chuckled. "But if she did, I'd consider my fate worth it for a kiss with you."

"Don't do it again."

"Why not? You didn't like it?"

"I am an unwed maiden and as such, I am off-limits to all affections from men…and that includes you." She pulled away, surprised that he let her unpeel from his embrace. "You should remember that, King Ravn."

There was no smart reply, no disagreement, but she felt the heat of his gaze as she made her way past the rowers and sat back down beside the mast. Once again, she hugged her knees and pulled her hood up, losing herself in a dark, little cave.

But when she closed her eyes, all she could think of was his lips on hers, the feel of his arms surrounding her like a great fortress wall that would keep her safe.

She knew what happened between married men and women—she had a married friend at court who had been happy to fill her in one evening after some potent fortified wine. But still, Carmel struggled to imagine the act, and imagining it with a man like Ravn was impossible.

Or was it?

An image of him chopping wood with his torso naked came to mind. His strength and vigor was almost divine. She wondered what he'd be like without any clothes. With his cock thick and erect, as her friend had described it would be when aroused and ready for the marital bed.

A shiver snaked up through her belly and seemed to tug at her nipples. These were not the thoughts of a good Christian woman. She should be ashamed of herself.

She *was* ashamed of herself.

THEY TRAVELED FOR three weeks, stopping at land twice to restock the longboat with fresh water, mead, and food. Each time, Carmel stayed aboard and didn't speak to anyone. She just waited while Ravn and the crew bartered in their native tongue.

She'd stayed distant from Ravn, barely speaking to him, not wanting to put herself in a position where he could kiss her again. She might be a long way from a church, but God could still see her.

As she'd sat being gently rocked, her grief gripped her in its mean fist. Tears fell for her father, for the young men who'd fallen around him. Her anger at Haakon rose and fell like a series of waves. They'd attacked Tillicoulty, and they'd gotten more than they'd bargained for. Whose fault was that?

Her mother's face hovered before her. Her father's also.

Would she ever see her brother again? Perhaps when he was a grown man, he would come and find her. If she survived that long.

Eventually, they sailed between two vast, snow-topped mountains that were lined with waterfalls and littered with brave little trees rooting into the rocks. Turning east, they drifted onto a still and silent fjord. The Vikings stopped rowing and sat still and quiet, their oar handles resting on their laps.

Overhead, a bird of prey called and in the distance, rising from mist, was a crescent beach with a pier lined with longboats and alight with flaming iron baskets. Beyond it, the many pitched roofs of Drangar spread toward a cleft in the mountains.

"Home," Ravn said after a few minutes. "Thanks be to all the gods for our safe arrival."

Carmel crossed herself. They'd been lucky. The weather had been kind to them with only a few days of rain, no storms, and waves the boat handled with ease.

As they drew closer, the Vikings began to row again, slicing through the water as though it were butter on a hot day.

A drum sounded, its thick beat echoing around the valley.

"Ha, they have seen us." Ravn stood at the prow, his cloak flicking behind him in the breeze. "We will feast tonight, men, and we will deserve every mouthful of food and swallow of ale."

A cheer went up.

Carmel tightened her cloak and tried to beat down nerves. It was hard not to feel like she was being lowered into a pit of vipers. If Orm was anything to go by, the townsfolk of Drangar could be terrifying.

They were met with a crowd at the pier. Smiles and waves and shouts of *"Konge Ravn! Konge Ravn!"* Flags flapped and dogs barked. The drum sounded louder and a banner with the image of a black raven was hoisted high up a pole.

"My good people. Your king has returned!" Ravn shouted.

Men rushed to secure the boat, and the crew leaped out and were absorbed by the crowd as they found their families.

"Princess, your hand." Ravn stooped to look under her hood at her face.

She shook her head, wishing she could become invisible.

"Your hand," he repeated, taking it. "The people of Drangar will want to meet their new princess."

"I am not a princess here."

"You are *my* princess." He grinned. "And they will treat you as such." He tipped closer. "That is my promise."

She pulled in a breath as the shouts and cheers grew louder still.

"Come on. We have been on this boat long enough. It is time to find our land legs again."

"Our what?"

He laughed. "You will see what I mean." He pulled her to standing and circled her waist as though expecting her to topple overboard.

The roar of the crowd was deafening as they stepped onto the pier. She kept her hood pulled up, overwhelmed by the surge of strangers.

The moment her feet hit the wooden boards, Carmel knew what Ravn had referred to.

Her knees were weak, her legs shaky. It was as though she were still compensating for the rocking of the boat, yet the surface beneath her was unmoving.

"Oh," she said, clinging to the sleeve of his tunic. "This is…peculiar."

"It can take a day or two." He grinned then lifted his hand into the air. For a few minutes, he spoke loudly in his native tongue.

She looked around at the posse of Viking men and women. They were all tall and strong, their clothes hardy and decorated with brooches and chains. She barely saw anyone without a weapon at their belt. Even the youngest boys had knives sheathed at their waist.

"I have just informed them that you are with me and are of

royal blood from a land far away," he said. "They will respect you."

"Are you sure?" She caught the eye of a woman who had ink down one side of her face, a detailed pattern that reminded Carmel of a tangle of ivy.

"*Ja*, I am sure." He squeezed her closer. "Where is thrall Joseph?" he called.

There was movement in the crowd. "I am here, Your Grace." An aging man with curly, gray hair, clean-shaven, and with deep-brown eyes stepped forward. He wore a dark fur around his shoulders that was secured with a strip of leather at his chest.

"Ah, good." Ravn clasped him on the shoulder. "Meet Princess Carmel. She speaks your tongue, so you will ensure she understands what others are saying to her."

"I will translate, aye." He tipped his head and studied her. "I trust you had a good journey, Your Highness."

"As well as can be expected." She paused. "You are a slave here, I have been told."

"Slave?" He paused. "No, I work here in Drangar, for the king and his family."

"But where are you from? Where is home?"

He laughed. "This is home now. I have forgotten about my old one."

"The one you were taken from against your will." She folded her arms and studied him.

"I guess that's how it happened, yes." Joseph shrugged.

"Mmm, I see the king's family has a history of kidnapping." She tipped her eyebrows at Ravn. "Father and now son."

Ravn laughed. "I have a history of many things. Some I might tell you about. Some I might not."

She scowled at him. "Your father took a man of God."

Joseph rubbed his head as though remembering his tonsure. "It was God's will that I live this life now."

"With heathens?"

"With heathens." Joseph grinned. "Shall I show you where

you can bathe, Princess? I am sure after weeks at sea, a hot bath is just what you would enjoy."

"A hot bath?"

"Aye, the Vikings are very fond of hot baths. It is just one of the rituals I enjoy now that I live a new life."

"Joseph, there you are. Oh, and King Ravn, welcome home, Your Grace." A pretty woman with hair in long braids appeared at Joseph's side.

"Thank you, Erin." Ravn nodded at her. "This is my princess, Carmel. I trust you will look after her and speak in the language Joseph has taught you, as it is hers too."

"Of course, Your Grace." Erin gave a funny little bow. "Welcome, Princess."

"I allowed Joseph to marry Erin before I left for Tillicoulty," Ravn said. "He wouldn't take her to his bed until he did and it has been so many years, he has wanted to. That strange Christian tradition of yours."

"You are married?" Carmel raised her eyebrows. "But you are a monk, are you not? How can you be married?"

"I am not a monk." Joseph shrugged. "At least not anymore."

She crossed herself. "What devil place have I come to where monks marry?"

"Don't look so miserable," Erin said. "You might just enjoy it."

Carmel huffed. She very much doubted that.

Chapter Ten

CARMEL STARED AROUND the grand home that belonged to King Ravn. It was twice the size of the Great House in Tillicoulty. Long and with shutters that could be opened and closed during the seasons. A lengthy fire trough glowed with embers and the room was sectioned into what appeared to be a feasting area, a food preparation area, and a sleeping area.

There was also a screened section—thin branches wound tightly—that contained a fire and a large low barrel that was half full with water. The wall beside it was crowded with baskets, strips of fabric, and ropes of drying herbs.

"The season is on the turn and the weather warming," Erin said, bustling past her with a stack of logs in her arms. "So the fires are not lit constantly."

Carmel nodded.

Erin stooped beside the barrel and began stacking kindling and logs for a fire. "But we must light one now to warm the water."

"'Water'?"

"For you to bathe. The king will want to also."

"He can use the bath." She stepped away from it. "It is his home. It is his bath."

"It is yours also." Erin looked up at her. "That was his specific instruction to me, that you must feel at home here."

"But I…" She frowned. "Surely, he means for me to sleep somewhere else. In another dwelling."

"His wife, who is now in Valhalla feasting with Freya after dying in the battle of childbirth, slept in here, so why shouldn't you?"

A shocked laugh escaped Carmel. "Because I am not his wife."

Erin smiled up at her and scraped a flint. "No, you are not."

"I cannot sleep in here."

"Why not? It is the grandest dwelling in Drangar. The walls are solid, the floor well covered with rugs, and the beds are freshly made and warm."

"'Beds'?"

"*Ja*, there are several."

She nodded and noticed that through a doorway was a large bed covered in white furs, but also to the left was a small cot, similar to the one she'd used in Orm's little home.

Erin saw her looking. "That is Thormod's cot."

"His son?"

"*Ja*. Though he spends a lot of time with Helga and his cousins, especially now that the king has taken to raiding again."

"He didn't raid on this mission." Carmel frowned. "It was peaceful."

"No?"

"No."

"So what are you?" She paused as the fire sprang to life. "If not the fruits of his pillaging."

"I am not an object. I was not pillaged."

Erin didn't answer. She lifted a huge pot of water over the fire and added several long strands of lavender to it. "This will take a while to heat. Then we can add it into the barrel. I will go and fetch you some food. You must be hungry."

She left Carmel alone in the large home that smelled of smoke and ash, and herbs and leather. She walked around it, her legs still feeling odd, and studied a table holding several pieces of jewelry. She picked up a brooch in the shape of a wolf's head, the eye a small, amber gem. Next she examined a necklace, the silver thick and heavy, the pendant a series of triangles set into each other and with another amber gem in the center. Had they belonged to Ravn's wife? Were they the adornments of a dead woman?

She moved to the right and came face to face with a large, stone statue clutching what looked like a bulky hammer. It had an angular square chin and narrowed eyes. At its base were several skeletons and a scattering of coins.

What was it?

"Thor."

She gasped and turned around.

Ravn stood there, hands on his hips, feet apart, the shadows of the room dancing on his face and dark beard. "That is Thor's image and a place for sacrifices to be made to him."

She turned again to the skeleton. It looked like a rat. "You make sacrifices, here, in your home, to your gods?" The idea seemed particularly savage.

"Of course. Don't you?"

"No." She removed her cloak, the room suddenly warm.

He took it and hung it on a hook to her right. "We make many sacrifices, especially at the great festival of Uppsalla," he said. "Every nine years, we make the pilgrimage there, on foot, and beside the ancient sacred tree Yggdrasil, nine sacrifices are made of animal and man."

"'Man'?" Her eyes widened. "You kill men as sacrifices?"

"It is a great honor." He walked to the water, setting another log on the flames beneath it. "To be chosen."

"It sounds terrible."

"Orm would agree with you."

"I don't understand."

He turned. "Orm was chosen as one of the human sacrifices, but he refused." Ravn's face tightened. "It brought great shame to my father, who never forgave him."

"But surely..." She held her hands out, palms up, the idea incomprehensible. "Surely, it was up to him. Orm's decision whether or not to die."

Ravn shrugged. "It was his decision to bring dishonor."

"But, Ravn." She stepped up to him. "Life is God's precious gift to us, all of the gods' gift to us. Surely, they don't want us to die? Surely, they want us to live good lives in the service of others."

"It is how we think differently. My gods await me to sup with them in Valhalla, to feast afresh each day on the most succulent meats and delicious fruit. It is an eternity I look forward to."

"We really do think differently." She turned, her hands clasped in prayer. What if they decided to sacrifice her to their big, stone god?

"Maybe one day you will understand," he said, coming up behind her. Close, the way he had on the ship when they'd seen the delfins.

"I'm not sure I *want* to understand. Why would you want to be without your brother? I care for mine and wish him well."

"You have met him. Orm."

"Aye, and I can't say I like him, but it's a special bond between brothers, isn't it?" She paused and closed her eyes. "Unless he has always been jealous of you and Haakon."

"'Jealous'?"

She turned and smiled up at his confused expression. "You are not like other brothers. You are not only twins, you are both powerful kings. You are both…"

"What?" He lowered his head a little.

Words tumbled around her mind. Brave. Handsome. Strong. Determined. But did she want to say them aloud and let Ravn known her thoughts on him?

"Tell me what you think of me?" he said quietly. "I want to know."

"Why?" She swallowed and tried to tear her attention from his lips, which only reminded her of her first kiss.

"Because I am not a mind reader," he said. "I wish to know your opinion of me now that you are safely arrived in Drangar."

"Well." She straightened her shoulders. "That is good that you are not a mind reader, because it is not one of the things I would use to describe you." She stepped past him.

"So what words would you use?"

"At this point in time, smelly." She piled her hair on top of her head and wrinkled her nose.

"That is hardly my fault." He plucked at his tunic and sniffed. He wrinkled his own nose.

"I didn't say it was, but I am going to bathe first, as I was invited to, so if you would excuse me."

He followed her to the bathing area and leaned against a pillar, crossing one foot over the other, shoulder bunched on the wood. "This is my home. Why should I leave?"

"Because." She used a small pail to scoop up hot water. "You said I'd be happy here, and for that, I need privacy." She circled her finger in the warm water.

"You put a high price on your nakedness."

She hesitated, then, "I know you are a man of your word, Ravn. That is one way I'd describe you."

"I am!" He tilted his chin and straightened. "You are right. I am a man of my word."

She smiled.

"I will leave you to recover from the journey, Princess. And while you do that, I will visit my son." He turned and walked away.

She studied his broad back as he took long paces away from her. He was even more regal here in his own kingdom. He exuded the confident stance of a man with power and influence. He was also a man with a quest to atone for his wrongdoings. There was something about that which appealed to the Christian in her.

Perhaps there was hope for Ravn's soul.

She lingered in the hot water. Erin brought her ale and a platter of salted fish and pickles along with chestnut hair cleanser that lathered up wonderfully. Erin also brought clean clothes—

the first in weeks—and when Carmel had dried and brushed her hair, it was luxurious to slip into soft pants and a warm, woven woolen tunic the color of the yellow flowers at home.

"You know of the king's brothers and sister," Erin asked.

"Aye, I do."

"And what of them?"

"They are well. They are in the new kingdom of Tillicoulty."

"Is that where you are from?"

"Not exactly." She didn't elaborate. Erin was a stranger. "King Haakon has taken a wife."

"A crown and a wife." Erin smiled. "The gods have been kind to him."

"He appears happy."

"And what is his wife like?"

"Queen Kenna." Carmel thought for a moment. "She is kind, pretty of face, strong, so hopefully will bear him many sons."

"I am pleased for Haakon. He was always kind to everyone he met."

Carmel huffed. "Not if he met them on a battlefield."

"Well, no, obviously. But he's a warrior who demands victory. It is what he does. He defends what is his and takes what he wants. That is the path the gods set out for him."

Carmel again stayed quiet. She was a stranger in these lands. To confess that her father's army, with her in the wings, had attacked King Haakon could drop her in hot water of the unpleasant kind. "You are happy with Joseph? He is good to you?"

"*Ja*, he is a man I admire."

"Even though he is not from your lands."

"The seer told my mother, when I was just a young girl, that my destiny would come to me from over the sea." She stroked her belly. "That the fruits of my destiny would have blood that didn't start flowing in the Northlands the way mine did."

"You are…pregnant?"

Erin smiled. "I do not know for sure, but I hope so. I would like to give Joseph sons before he gets much older."

Carmel was quiet as Erin brushed her hair again. In her world, the thought of a monk having a wife and child was ludicrous. Yet here…in this cold, jagged land, it wasn't strange at all.

What else would she get used to before her mother's army saved her?

If they ever saved her.

"Why are you here?" Erin asked suddenly.

"Why am I here?"

"*Ja.*" She poured two jugs of ale. "What brought you to Drangar?"

"I had no choice."

"What did you have no choice in?" A deep voice came from behind her.

Carmel turned.

Ravn stood there holding a small boy with blond hair cut as though a round bowl had been put on his scalp and everything below it shaved off.

"To be here." She frowned.

"We all do things we have no choice in."

"Like what?"

"Remember the delfins." He bit his bottom lip and grinned. "I had no choice in doing something then. I was overcome with it."

Instantly, she knew he was talking about their kiss. It was the way he looked at her with an intensity that had heat flowing into her veins in the same way it had when he'd kissed her.

"How could I forget?" She turned away, her cheeks burning.

"This is my son, Thormod." He stooped and set the child down. "This will be his second summer."

"Thormod." Erin held out her arms to him. "Come. I have sweet rhubarb for you."

"Wait," Ravn said.

The child stopped and turned to his father with wide, blue eyes. "Say *hello* to Princess Carmel. Speak in the tongue of Joseph."

Thormod turned to Carmel as though seeing her for the first time. He wasn't shy. He stepped up close and peered at her eyes.

"Hello," she said. "What is this?" She pointed at the little, wooden toy in his hand.

"*Båt.*"

"Boat," Ravn corrected. "Speak your new mother's tongue."

Thormod's eyes widened and he turned to Ravn.

Carmel felt as shocked as little Thormod about the introduction but tried not to show it. "Can I see your boat?" she asked, forcing a smile.

He held it out to show her but didn't hand it over.

"It's a strong boat, good for big waves," she said with a serious nod.

He didn't speak and snatched the boat back to his chest.

"Come, Thormod. Let us find that rhubarb," Erin said. "And let your father and new mother rest after their long journey."

Quickly, Thormod turned and ran to Erin.

She hoisted him up into her arms. "I will take him until you ask for him or he asks for Helga."

"Thank you." Ravn nodded and stroked his son's hair, a tender gesture that had his features softening.

Erin left the dwelling.

"You missed him." Carmel nodded at the doorway.

"*Ja.* He is my son. My blood."

"He reminds me of my brother at that age. His hair was also the color of dawn light."

Ravn sat and shoved at his boots. They fell to the floor with two bangs and he left them lying. He then stood and pulled at his top, dropping it over his boots. "This tunic needs burning."

She didn't reply.

He pulled his belt free, dropping it down with a clunk as the axe and dagger hit the floor. "And these. Also for burning."

Next came his pants. He pushed them down his wide thighs, the left one dark with ink, and kicked them away.

Carmel gasped and spun around. "In God's name, what are

you doing?" The sight of his big cock flaccid against his dark body hair had made her heart skip a beat and shock rampage through her system.

"Bathing," he said. "Unlike you, I do not hold such a high price on my naked body."

She heard the slosh of water and his deep sigh of bliss.

Without a word, she walked past the fire trough, the statue of Thor, and into the bed area. She lay on the thick, white furs, drew up her knees, and closed her eyes.

Sleep. She needed sleep.

And if she prayed hard enough, maybe she'd wake up in her castle and this would all be a bad dream.

Chapter Eleven

RAVN CLOSED HIS eyes, sank down, and let the water circle his neck. He'd been dreaming of a soak in hot water for days. He hadn't expected it to smell of rosemary, but he wasn't complaining. The smell would always remind him of Carmel.

Carmel.

What game were the gods playing to set out his fate with a Christian woman? A princess, at that.

He didn't want to want her.

Hadn't planned on bringing a woman back to Drangar.

But here she was. In his home. Looking like a shiny berry ripe for plucking. With wit, compassion, and wisdom and a way of looking at him like she saw something good there—and not just the bad blood he'd become used to thinking flowed in his veins. He couldn't stop thinking about her.

But she'd been so quiet on the boat. Tortured by her grief. Something he thanked the gods he had not had a hand in. She could blame Haakon, Astrid, and Orm for that. He'd left her to her melancholy knowing that time was a healer and these things couldn't be rushed.

And that kiss. Also not planned. But he hadn't been able to help himself. He'd had no choice but to press his lips to hers. She'd been irresistible. He'd been expecting a swift slap or tart remark, but nothing had come and he'd lost himself in her for a few sweet moments marveling at the fact a woman could make his heart beat so fast.

His cock grew hard and he reached for it, the water splashing slightly. An image of Carmel naked and waiting for his kisses came to mind. She was small and light with curves in the places he liked to see a woman's curves. And she was untouched. A virgin.

His belly tensed and his erection thickened in his fist. He rubbed it root to tip and his balls tightened.

What would it take to be the first man to enter her?

Sure, he could do it by force. He was twice the size of her and she was effectively his captive.

But he shuddered just at the thought of the pain and disappointment in her eyes. He'd never violate her like that.

No. He wanted her wet and willing and open for him. *Begging* for him.

His cock twitched and he stroked it some more, imagining her reaching for him and bringing him to full hardness. Her sweet, small hands exploring, teasing and pleasuring. The look on her face as he taught her the wonders of building to an orgasm and then experiencing the climax itself.

Oh, and he'd have her cumming that first time. He was good at sex—he'd been told that often enough. True, some areas of his life he'd been accused of being selfish, but not when it came to sweaty, naked time. Then he wanted his woman, or women, to be crying his name as they pulsed around his cock or dragged on his hair as his tongue worked.

He moaned softly and the urge to find pleasure right there in the water almost took him over. But he resisted, and instead, he dunked under, scrubbing at his hair to get rid of the layers of salt the sea breeze had basted there.

After a while, the water cooled and he stepped out, dried, and pulled on fresh pants. He didn't bother with his belt or a tunic. He needed to sleep. The rock and roll of the longboat had meant for broken rest in between taking his turn at rowing.

He rubbed a piece of linen over his hair to dry it then sat beside a bowl of water and took his sharp, iron razor in his hand.

After lathering, he began to shave his beard away.

As the clumps of hair came off, the beads with it, he felt lighter, renewed. As though he were leaving the past behind.

When it was all off and his skin smooth, he rinsed and patted his face dry.

He supped ale and ate salted fish then headed for his bed.

Carmel was on it. She was lying on her side, curled into a ball and apparently fast asleep.

His cock stirred again. If ever there were an invitation to take what he wanted, there it was.

"Fuck it," he muttered, reaching for a wolf fur.

He covered her, then gently lay on the bed at her side. His arms ached to hold her, nestle her against his body and inhale the scent of her hair, but he stopped himself. Instead, he fastened his hands behind his head, stared at the beamed ceiling, and waited for sleep.

It came quickly and soon, dreams of Tillicoulty and his brothers and Astrid filled his mind. Thormod was there too, but as a baby, not a toddling child. Thor loomed over them, hammer in hand, and delfins dived through the air at his side.

And then the familiar scent of chestnut soap filled his nose; it was laced with lavender and penetrated his dreams.

He stirred and was aware of a weight over him. His arms were full and his legs tangled in fur and legs.

He opened his eyes.

Carmel was sprawled out on him, almost as though he were a pillow. Her head was nestled in the crook of his shoulder. She had one hand on his chest and her legs were entwined with his. Her breath warmed his flesh.

He froze, not wanting to break the spell. Had he reached for her or had she navigated his way?

From what he could figure out, he'd barely moved and was still on his back on the side of the bed he'd started on.

And then she stirred, a little squeak and a sigh as she arched her back and her fingers curled in the hair at the center of his chest. Tugging it just enough to invoke a pleasurable sting.

He hardly dared breathe and kept a tight hold of her in the circle of his arm.

"What the…?" She lifted her head and stared at him, blinking a few times, then her eyes widened.

"I… I didn't do this… You came to me," he said, wondering if she was about to fall into a hysteria.

"I…" She looked at her hand filled with his dark curls of chest hair and then back at his face. "I'm sorry." Her fingers relaxed.

"Don't be sorry."

She was staring at him as if she'd never seen him before.

It was then he remembered. "Ah, I shaved." He stroked his chin.

"You look different."

"In a good or bad way?"

"I like it." She lifted her hand and with her index finger traced his jawline very slowly, right to his chin and then back to his left ear.

Fuck. His cock twitched and heat rushed to his lower belly. Her touch was magic. "That's good." He wanted to trace her face, learn every curve and dip of her entire body. "That you like it."

"Why does it matter what I think?"

He hesitated then, "I want you to like me."

"Why?"

"Because I like you." The words gushed from him. "A lot."

"You stole me away from my homeland, Ravn. Why would I ever like you?" Her words were harsh, but her eyes and the tone of her voice soft.

"Because I saved you from a life as my brother's slave. Because I have brought you to a place that will expand your mind like no other and when you return to your homeland, you will have so many sagas to tell, your name will be famous and your wisdom sought."

"'When I return to my homeland.'" She pressed her palm to his cheek. "Is that what you just said?"

"*Ja.*"

"When?"

He thought for a moment. "I will take you in three summers if you still want to go. The fallout from the battle will be over, Tillicoulty will be an established kingdom, and your young brother old enough to negotiate with should I need to."

"Three summers?"

He frowned. "Is that too long?"

"No." She shook her head. "Not when I thought it would be never. Three summers, I can do."

"Here. With me?"

"Aye, here with you." She leaned up and pressed her lips to his.

It was so unexpected, his eyes stayed wide and for a second, he froze.

Almost immediately, she pulled back. "I'm… I'm sorry. I—"

He cupped his hand around her nape and pulled her in for another kiss. This time, he took control, gently teasing her response and touching his tongue to hers.

She moaned softly and he rolled her over so she was beneath him. He was careful to take his weight. He didn't want to crush her.

"I want you," he said, not bothering to hide the need in his voice. The desire in his eyes spoke volumes; there was no disguising it now.

"I know, but you can't have me. Not willingly."

She pushed his hair from his face with both of her hands. The tender gesture had his cock rising to full length. She was a conundrum, a complex twist of yes and no.

"Why can't I? I am king. I can have what I want."

"And I am a Christian woman who cannot bed a man who is not my husband."

"We will wed today."

A brief smile flashed over her mouth as though amused by his urgency.

"What? Is that funny?" he asked.

"You do not want to marry me. I am your thrall."

"You are my princess and I will make you my queen."

"Your people will not accept it."

"They will do as they are told. I will make them accept it. If they don't, they will be punished."

"Is that how you intend to go through life? As a dictator?" She paused and a slight frown appeared, as though a memory had come to her. "A king who punishes anyone who does not agree with you?"

He wasn't sure how to answer that. Wasn't that how a king should be? Yet there was a warning in her eyes that he'd better answer the correct way. "Do you want me to be a dictator?"

"No." She pushed at him. "Of course not." She wriggled free and slipped from the bed.

He sat, hands up, as though in surrender. "What did I do wrong?"

"You can't just announce you're going to marry me."

"Why not? You came to me in bed last night. *My* bed. Surely, that proves you want me."

She placed her hands on her hips. "I was asleep. That is all. I didn't know what I was doing."

"You did when you kissed me just then."

"Ravn." She stepped up to him and cupped his face, staring down at him. "You have an inherent distaste for Christendom. I have seen your disapproval of Haakon marrying Kenna and converting to God's flock. You are not Christian and you do not want to be. It could never be between us."

"I understand it now. I was hasty back then."

"What do you understand?"

"That all of our gods, yours and mine, weave our paths together. They are one and the same."

"There is only one God. My God."

"Do not disrespect Thor and Odin and the gods who feast with them."

"I apologize." She straightened and stepped away. "Truly."

He said nothing.

"There must be a woman here in Drangar who would serve you better as your wife. A woman who knows the Viking ways and who can be a good mother to Thormod."

"There is no woman here for me." He thought of Helga and how he'd told her that she'd never be his queen despite her obvious desire for him. He just hadn't felt the same. "That is why my destiny set me on a path to Tillicoulty. That is why your destiny also took you there, to a village that was not yours. So that our paths would cross, so that you would come here and help me be a better king."

"A better king?"

"I need your gentle wisdom." He stepped closer, sensing she wasn't about to bolt or slap him and her irritation was calming. "I admire your thoughts, your ideas. You are a worthy queen and I would be proud to have you at my side."

"Ravn." Her eyes misted a little. "But…"

"There is no *but*."

She fingered the cross on her earring and looked at the floor.

"Carmel," he whispered, raising her face. "Would you really rather live as a slave than a queen while you are here?"

"No…" She shook her head. "But how can I go home in three years if I am your wife?"

"I will let you go." His mouth fastened into a tight line. "If I have to."

She swallowed. Did he mean divorce? If so, that wasn't something she believed in…until now, perhaps.

"In that time, I promise to respect your god, even though I am not Christian," he said. "That is the best I can do."

"And I will respect yours."

"Then that is settled. We will marry." He saw a flash of fear in her eyes and hated that it was there. "Tell me. What scares you?"

"I… I… I am a virgin and you are… And I don't think I can…"

"What?"

"I don't think a woman from my lands can bed a man from the north. It will not work. You are too big."

A burst of laughter came from him. "That is what worries you?"

She frowned. "It is more than a worry. It is a truth."

"Then how do you think Haakon and Kenna do it?"

"I…" She frowned. "I don't know. I hadn't thought about it. That would be wrong."

"Well, think about this: not only is Haakon a Norseman, he also has an iron piercing through his cock."

Her mouth fell open. "Lord have mercy on his soul. That cannot be true."

"It is. I swear on Thor's hammer it is."

"It is impossible."

"It is not. Though I do not have such a thing, so consider yourself lucky if that is something that scares you."

"'Lucky'?" She screwed up her eyes. "Please, can I wake up from this nightmare?"

Ravn couldn't help but feel offended. "I have just asked you to be my queen and you think you are in a nightmare."

"Do you know me so little?"

"I know you. And I know you are resilient, and brave, and that you will do the right thing. You will take the path your god has set out for you." He wrapped his arms around her and snapped her close. "I believe in you."

She gasped and placed her hands on his bare chest, staring up at him.

"Now say you will wed me this day and let's be done with it." Her petite body felt so good pressed up against him. As though they were meant to be.

"Wed you this day and bed you this night?"

"*Ja*, and…" He pulled in a deep breath and lowered his voice. "I will give you my word it will be a night you remember for all the right reasons. It will be full of pleasure and satisfaction. Every desire will be fulfilled, every need met." He paused, enjoying the rising flush on her cheeks and her shallow, rapid breaths. She was hanging on to his every word. "I will make you feel more adored than you ever have before. I will show you how real men pleasure a woman. I will show you that you will never want to leave me once I have made you cry out my name in ecstasy over and over again. It will be the most perfect night in the mortal world."

"You can certainly…" She cleared her throat. "Talk the talk."

"Trust me, I can walk the walk too." He set his mouth over hers.

Chapter Twelve

CARMEL PULLED BACK from the heated kiss and stared up at Ravn. With his new clean-shaven jawline and his freshly washed hair, he looked almost civilized.

Almost.

But that was beside the point. It was his words, his filthy, seductive, delicious, and terrifying words that were rattling around her mind and making her heart beat so fast, she feared for its survival.

Wed.

Be his queen.

If he hadn't looked so serious, she'd have thought he was jesting.

And there was no denying he was real. This was no dream. His big, hard, hot body pressed against the length of hers. His hair-coated flesh smelled of soap and sleep and his eyes bored into her soul.

"I will wed you," she said, hardly believing the words that were coming from her mouth. But he was right. Being a queen was preferable to a thrall for the next three years. "On one condition."

"Anything." He ran his hands down her back as though learning her shape. "I will do anything for you."

"If we have children in this marriage, they are raised Christian." *And,* she promised herself, *they will return to Lothlend with me.*

His eyebrows lowered and his jaw tensed.

"I am not saying they will not know Thor and Odin and all of your gods," she went on, "but they must know mine. Our savior Jesus Christ must be in their lives." For a moment, she thought he'd refuse. That he'd change his mind about marrying her and stomp off.

But then his face softened. "They will have broad minds with a good understanding of the world." He nodded slowly. "So when they raid, they will know the value of what they are pillaging from Christians."

"Well..." She frowned thinking of the Commandments and how her father hadn't stuck to them as well as he should have. All of her life, she'd believed in his divine right to tax and battle, but perhaps he could have been a more benevolent ruler of his people. "I will be sure to teach them that taking what isn't theirs is sinful."

Suddenly, he picked her up and spun her around.

She gasped and clutched his shoulders. "Ravn."

"I will announce our marriage to the villagers. They will not be surprised." He grinned. "They will be joyful. A great feast will be prepared and I will send Erin to help you get ready."

"'Get ready'?"

"*Ja*. A bride must get ready for her new husband." He swept his lips over her lips. "A new queen must get ready to formally meet her new people."

CARMEL SPENT THE day with Erin and two other women who didn't speak her language. Several of their children milled about Ravn's home, including Thormod, who was more interested in playing with his boat in a pail of water than engaging with her.

"He still cries for his mother," Erin said as she brushed Carmel's hair. "But less now than at the beginning."

"It is a terrible thing to lose a parent, whatever age."

"*Ja*, my mother also went last winter. The fever that swept through the village after Haakon left was vicious. Some said it was the gods' doing, that they were angered at the way the brothers had fought for power."

"Power is a seductive thing. Blinding to some." Had her father been blinded by it?

Erin was quiet for a moment as one of the women passed her a tiny, white flower with a delicate stalk. Carefully, she pinned up a plaited loop of Carmel's hair onto the crown of her head and secured the flower within it.

The other woman held up a long, linen dress. It was the color of a summer sky, the neckline square, and it was embellished with exquisite golden embroidery. A thick leather belt had been attached to the waist so that it cinched in.

"What do you think?" Erin asked.

"Is that for me?"

"*Ja*, it has never been worn before. You will be the first."

"It's… It's beautiful."

"I am glad you like it." Erin continued to add flowers to her hair. "Ravn is different upon his return to Drangar."

"He is? How?"

"He has smiled." She laughed. "That never used to happen."

"Really?" When Carmel thought of Ravn, she pictured him with a smile on his face. Either that or with lust in his eyes. "Why didn't it?"

"I have no knowledge of that, but I can guess it was his desire to be king over his brother." She hesitated. "Orm always annoyed him too. Do you know Orm?"

"Oh, aye, I know Orm. And he annoys me also." Carmel laughed and was glad there was an ocean between her and Orm.

"The gods were playing a strange game when they created him."

"It is true Orm is different," Carmel said. "Though I think…"

"What?"

"I think there is a woman in Tillicoulty who is rather fond of him."

"Really? That is good. I have seen him enjoy naked pleasure, but never with the same woman for long."

Carmel felt her cheeks heating at the mention of sex. She dipped her head.

"Are you looking forward to your wedding night?"

"Why would you ask that?" Wasn't such a topic rather personal?

"Ravn is a hot-blooded man. He will take a woman with much passion. You are not marrying a virgin the way I did." Erin paused. "Not to mention, the king looks at you as though he were starving and you are a delicious meal that he cannot wait to devour."

Her belly twisted over itself and she gulped. "All I can do is hope he can control his appetite."

Erin laughed. "Oh, honey, why would you want him to?"

A FEW HOURS later, Carmel stood on the pier with Erin at her side and Ravn before her.

A crowd stood on the beach and looked on. The fire cages had been lit and the longboats bobbed on a gentle swell.

"Take each other's hands," Joseph said, holding up a length of silky, blue material.

Ravn gently took her hand. His mouth was a solemn, straight line and his hair plaited neatly. He wore a brass crown dotted with amber. His gray tunic had brown leather strapping that crossed at his chest and was studded with bronze. Leather also wrapped around the lower half of the sleeves and his pants and boots matched. He was tall and regal and the sword at his belt glinted in the sunshine.

"May all the gods, the mighty All Father and God in heaven,

look upon you today with joy and offer you prosperity and good fortune." Joseph wrapped the silk ribbon around their wrists three times, then he tied a knot, binding them together. "In the exchanging of words and swords, you will now become man and wife and forever walk the paths of destiny and fate together."

Carmel's heart rate picked up as a gust of breeze caught a tendril of her hair. This really was it. She was to be wed. And in a way—and to a man—she could never have imagined.

"Princess Carmel," Ravn said, his concentration solely on her. "As your husband, I pledge to cherish, honor, and respect you from this day until my last. I promise to protect you, to be loyal to you so that you forever know that you can always rely upon my heart, as it beats for you."

Her throat dried and a tremble went up her spine and over her scalp.

"Princess," Joseph said gently.

She pulled in a breath. "I stand before God Almighty and you, King Ravn of Drangar, on this day to pledge my devotion as a wife and mother to your children." She paused.

He squeezed her hand.

"And in the name of Jesus Christ my savior, I promise to honor and respect you, cherish you and forsake all others so that you are the only man in my heart." The words came out easier than she'd expected and she'd managed to hold in the fact that it would only be for three years.

A round of three seasons, that was all she had to commit to, then she would be free to live a chaste life as a divorcee back in Lothlend.

"And now for the exchanging of swords." Joseph handed a small, silver sword to Carmel.

She took the ornate handle and passed it to Ravn. He handed her his heavy one, which she held vertically with the point pressing into the wooden floor of the pier.

"And now"—Joseph held up his hands—"you are King and Queen of Drangar and husband and wife."

The crowd cheered and clapped and a drum banged loudly.

"Queen Carmel," Ravn said, snatching her close. "My beautiful wife, your people adore you, as do I."

His lips hit down on hers as his arms held her tightly. She could practically taste his desire; his need was hot and urgent. She dropped the sword and gripped the leather straps that went over his shoulders. She was glad he was holding her up. Her knees had become so weak.

A shower of tiny, white petals rained down on them and burning sage wafted around them.

"We will feast," Ravn said against her lips. "And then we can be alone."

"Ravn." She touched his cheek. "I…"

"What?"

"It is nothing." She shook her head and pressed her legs together. The thought of what was coming was terrifying. She'd have to pray and hope it was quick and that she wouldn't bleed too much afterwards or be in unbearable pain.

"Your day is only going to get better." He turned to the crowd and raised their joined hands. "My good people, my wife and I invite you to feast with us, to drink with us, and enjoy good music with us."

Tables and benches had been set up along the narrow beach and were stacked with fish and bread and buttered vegetables. Several great vats of stew sat over fires and the herby scent filled the air.

"Your Grace," Erin said, holding out a chair for Carmel.

"Thank you." Carmel sat and looked down the table.

The villagers were raucous and excitable. They raised their ale, shouting,

"*Skål, skål!*" Many turned her way as Ravn moved up the line clasping shoulders and accepting congratulations. Or at least that was what she presumed was happening, though some of the leers from men made her wonder just what had been said.

Erin passed her a plate of eggs and green vegetables along

with a goblet of fruit wine. "The men of the village approve of their new queen."

"What do they say?"

Erin laughed. "They say you have breasts as round as turnips and a backside as firm as a young filly's and you are sure to have a cunny as sweet a ripe fig."

"What?" Carmel covered her gaping mouth. "What truly awful…sinful things to say."

"It is a compliment." Erin laughed and supped her own wine. "Viking men have a way with words, no?"

"No." She took a gulp of wine. "I don't think they do."

Ravn sat next to her and hoisted Thormod, who was chewing on a chunk of bread, onto his lap. "Eat," he said, pointing to her plate. "You will need energy for later."

Nerves wound around her yet again and she picked up the egg and nibbled it.

"Look!" Ravn suddenly pointed upward. "Odin watches over this auspicious day."

A great flock of black birds, ravens, were flying overhead. They'd come from the direction of the fjord and were low and swift, their beating wings creating a low hum. There were so many, as they crossed directly over the feasting villagers, the birds cast a dark shadow onto the beach.

"It is a good omen," Erin said, "that Odin celebrates with you, King Ravn."

Ravn banged his chest. "Now I know for sure that the gods favor me once again. I took risks to step back onto the path of my destiny but it has paid off and here I am, prosperous and happy." He reached for Carmel's hand. "And with a beautiful new queen at my side."

Chapter Thirteen

THE FEASTING WENT on until dusk painted the sky lilac and
pink. The air cooled and an owl called from the shadows of
the forest.

Carmel spotted a woman in the crowd of revelers, long,
blonde hair loose and her eyes darting constantly Carmel's way.
After a while, she spoke to Joseph. "Who is that?"

"Who?"

"The pretty woman. She keeps staring at me."

"That is Helga." He paused. "Take no notice."

"What do you mean?"

He cleared his throat.

"Joseph?"

"You won't want to hear it," said the thrall.

"But I command it." She was sure she'd heard the name before.

"Of course, Your Grace." He inclined his head. "She was your
husband's bed companion and a carer for little Thormod this past
winter gone, after he lost Queen Siggy."

"Oh, I see." She looked at Helga anew. This was a woman
who had bedded her husband. Knew what that entailed. Survived.
"And she resents me being here?"

"No." Joseph shook his head. "She told me she admires your
bravery for completing such a journey and she envies your
beauty."

"She said that?"

"Those very words." He smiled gently. "Do not fear. You have no rivals here. This is your home now."

She looked at Ravn, suddenly curious to see if his attention should stray to Helga's. It didn't. He appeared oblivious of her as he spoke loudly to his companions at the table and called for more mead.

"Your Grace," Erin said, leaning close, her shoulder brushing Carmel's. "Shall I help you prepare for bed?"

Carmel gulped. Just the thought of bedtime—bedtime with Ravn—had her stomach clenching. "No, thank you. I can manage."

"Are you sure?"

"Aye, this is something I must bear alone."

Erin smiled. "I think you will find it takes two. And you won't have to bear it. You'll enjoy it, not least because your husband is a fine king."

Carmel didn't answer. Instead, she stood, brushed a few crumbs from her dress, and took a deep breath.

Several heads turned her way. The hum of conversation dulled. More people's attention landed on her.

"How do I say *thank you* in your language?" she asked Ravn.

"*Takk skal du ha.*"

She tilted her chin and pasted a smile on her face. "*Takk skal du ha.*"

"To our new queen. *Skål!*" Joseph shouted, raising his horn of ale. "All hail Queen Carmel."

"*Skål.* Queen Carmel." The crowd cheered.

Carmel ducked her head in acknowledgment and stepped away from the table.

Ravn caught her wrist, halting her. "I will come to you soon. Be ready for me."

The sudden urge to run into the forest came over her.

"Be ready," he said again.

The dark glint in his eyes and the deep timber in his voice screamed need and want and lust. He was a man who wouldn't be denied what he'd been waiting for.

"I am your queen." She pressed her lips together and pushed down the urge to seek out shadows and solitude. "I will be waiting for you."

"Good." He released her wrist and reached for his mead again. "And remember, this is the first night of many that I will take you."

Which was exactly what she feared. Stepping away from the table, she held up the hem of her gown and trudged her way across the beach. Some of the villagers were roaming around, children were playing, but they all stopped and looked at her with intense curiosity.

She managed a smile, aware that the way Erin had piled her hair up looked something like a crown, and tried to maintain as regal an air as was possible when she felt like a virgin about to be sacrificed.

When she reached her new home, she pushed through the wooden door then shut it tight. Leaning her back on it, she blew out a breath. "Dear Lord, what path have you led me down? I hope you understand it, for I do not." She walked up to Thor and frowned at his stony face. "No doubt you are enjoying this, huh? Right up your ugly, pagan street." She pouted at him and walked toward the embers that glowed beneath a pot of warm water.

After washing her hands and face and rinsing her mouth, she removed her boots and went into the bedroom area. Thormod had left one of his wooden toy horses on the furs and she moved it to one side. Likely, he'd be looking for it the next day.

She paused at the end of the bed then dropped to her knees, hands clasped beneath her chin. "Now I lay me down to sleep, I pray the Lord my soul to keep. Thy love guard me through the night, and wake me with the morning light. Matthew, Mark, Luke, and John, bless the bed that I lie upon. There are four corners to my bed, four angels 'round my head, one to watch, and one to pray, and two to bear my soul away." She pulled in a deep breath, knowing she would need the protection more than ever. "Amen."

The door clicked open and then shut with a resounding *bang*. She stayed still, her knees pressing into the soft rug on the floor, and the noise echoing around her brain.

Ravn was here.

Here to take what now belonged to him.

Her.

Her heart squeezed and her breath caught in her throat. She could have sobbed, but she fought it back. In that moment, she'd rather have been going into battle without her spear than facing her new husband and his big, hungry cock.

"Lord, give me strength," she murmured.

"What are you doing?" Ravn asked.

"I am praying."

"For what?"

"For the Lord to protect my soul."

"You have *me* to protect you now."

She heard the soft clang of buckles, the *swoosh* of material, and then the bang of his boots as he removed his clothing.

She waited—waited for him to grab her, shove her legs apart, and take her. Ride her like a devil possessed until he filled her with his seed.

But he didn't. The water splashed. Another log landed on the fire and there was the crackle of sparks.

Still, she waited. Her pulse thudded in her ears. Her pussy quivered and a shiver attacked her entire body, rattling up her spine.

"Carmel."

She didn't trust herself to speak.

"Carmel. Stand up." His voice was firm, demanding obedience.

With shaking legs, she did as he'd asked and stood. Focusing on one section of fur—a piece with several dark strands in it—she bent over. Double. Then with a few tugs and flicks, she raised her gown up her legs and over her bare buttocks. Presenting herself to him with her gown pooled in the hollow of her back. Palms flat and fingers sinking into the thick pile.

She squeezed her eyes shut. The humiliation of baring her naked ass shred a dignity she'd always held dear.

"What are you doing?" he asked gruffly.

"I am ready for you, as you requested." The cool air washed over her buttocks. She hadn't realized how hot she was. She swallowed and waited for him to kick her ankles apart, shove his cock in deep and blast out his desire.

"Like that?" he asked.

"I may be a virgin, but I have been told this much." Oh, why couldn't he just get it over and done with?

"Carmel." He was behind her. She could feel his body heat and hear his breathing.

This was it. She braced for impact.

"Carmel, I am not a horse or a dog, or a pig or an elk, for that matter." He set his wide hands on her ass cheeks and squeezed her flesh almost to the point of pain.

She gasped and locked her knees. "Oh!"

"And much as I am tempted to fuck you like this, and I will at some point, this is not right for our wedding night." He squeezed her ass some more, pushed her forward, then pulled her back onto his cock. But it didn't penetrate. The heated shaft lay against the cleft of her ass.

"I… I don't know what you mean."

"You will." He reached for her and pulled her to standing. With her back to his naked chest and his cock lodged between them, he whispered, "I want to see your face when I am inside you. I *need* to see your face, to make sure I am getting it right for you." He turned her and crooked his finger beneath her chin. The hem of her gown fell around her ankles again. "Tonight is about you, not me."

"But I…" The reflection of the flames gave his eyes an ethereal glow. A few strands of his hair were damp from where he'd just washed and hung to the left of his temple.

"Carmel, I want you, my cock is already hard for you, but there is more to those words." He kissed the tip of her nose. "I want you to learn the pleasure a man and woman can find together. That is what I really want."

His hardness pressed against her. It was impossibly big and solid; she didn't dare look at it. "I can't imagine there will be any pleasure, just pain."

He frowned as though her words had pained him. "Do you have so little faith in your god?"

"I have ample faith."

"Then trust that he has made the joining of a man and woman pleasurable." He paused and ran his finger down her neck, to the hollow of her throat. "Do you trust me?"

"I want to," she said breathily.

"So do."

"I'll try."

"When the sun rises, you will understand what I mean about pleasure." He ran his fingers to the neckline of her dress. He traced it left to right, his touch a gentle caress. "But I can't tell you. I have to show you."

He lowered his head and kissed her. A gentle, unrushed kiss that created a strange longing inside her that wasn't at all unpleasant. If she did trust him, would she get more of that feeling? Would it grow?

She rested her hands on his bare chest and then found herself running her palms up his warm flesh to circle his neck. Despite her fears of being close to him, it felt right.

"You taste of everything I've ever needed," he murmured, kissing across her cheek. "I'm so thankful to have found you."

"Oh...Ravn."

She tipped her head back and he cradled the crown of her head and kissed down her neck. It was like having butterflies brushing against her. How could such a big man be so delicate?

"We need this off." He found the lacing on the back of her gown and undid it.

Immediately, the material loosened and then he stooped and gripped the hem, staring into her eyes he pulled it upward.

She was acutely aware that within seconds, she would be as naked as he and there would be no going back.

For a second, she was blinded by the wool and then she was in his arms. He pulled her close with one hand set over her ass and the other in the small of her back.

"You are mine to touch," he said, "as I am yours to touch."

Her hard nipples scraped against his chest.

"Hold me," he said, squeezing her closer still. "You must learn me as I learn you."

She bit on her bottom lip and stared into his eyes. Then she smoothed her hands from the rounds of his shoulders to his thick neck and then back down to his biceps. His flesh was warm and smooth and seemed to almost vibrate with the strength lurking beneath the surface.

He roamed his touch up her back, to her neck, then down to her ass again. He traced the shape of her waist and the flare of her hips.

Her breaths quickened and she ran her palms down his wide back to his ass. It was pleasingly taut and a sexy fuzz of hair covered each buttock.

Her breath hitched. Was this a sin? To enjoy a man's body this way?

"You're doing so well," he murmured, his lips almost touching hers. "And I like your hands on me."

"I'm glad."

"Touch me here too." He pulled back a fraction and took her right hand. He angled it between their bodies. "Touch my cock."

She gulped. "But shouldn't you just…"

"Shh, trust me, remember?"

She nodded and slipped lower into the warmth between their bodies. When she found his cock, she gasped at the size and steely hardness of it.

"Mmm." He closed his eyes. "Now hold it firm. Learn me."

For a moment, she hesitated, then, watching his rapt expression, she took it determinedly into her fist.

He groaned low and guttural.

She tightened her grip and ran her hand down to the base.

He groaned some more, a long expulsion of air.

"You like that?" she asked, hoping he did but not entirely sure.

"Fuck. *Ja*, I do." He opened his eyes and looked downward. "Your little hands on me... Fuck..."

She stroked him some more. His body tensed and his cock twitched within her hold. "Ravn."

"Carmel. So good...Mmm..." He cupped her face and pressed his lips to hers. His warm tongue probed and there was a little more urgency in his kiss than there had been before.

A flutter of excitement caught in her belly and she pressed her legs together as heat went to her pussy. Instead of feeling weak and overcome, as she'd expected, right now, she felt as though she held the reins. She was the one controlling his pleasure.

She ran her thumb over the tip of his cock, through the deep slit there. The glossy surface was a little damp.

"I don't want you to stop, but I think you should," he murmured, canting his hips for her touch.

"Why?" She held him firmer.

"Because it is not time for me to spill my seed yet." He suddenly caught her wrist, halting her movements. "And if you keep doing that, I will."

"Oh."

"Don't worry." He half-smiled. "You can play again later, as much as you want."

Before she could reply, he scooped her up. Next thing she knew, he was laying her on the soft furs that covered the bed. Her head sank into a feather pillow and he settled at her side.

"You have perfect breasts," he said, cupping the right one and squeezing it gently. "Look how they fit into my hand."

She didn't answer but watched him and concentrated on the

sensation of him caressing her breasts. Sighing, she closed her eyes.

And then her nipple was encased in wet heat. Opening her eyes, she saw that he'd taken it into his mouth.

"Ravn." She ran her hands onto his hair. "Oh, but… Oh, that feels…" She let out a moan that sounded more like a needy whimper. A need for more?

After a few minutes, he switched to the other breast. Her nipples were so hard and tingling, the weight of her breasts seeming to have increased. An aroused state of being had taken over her. Every patch of skin became more sensitive and between her legs, her pussy, there was a dragging, hot sensation that seemed to pulse with her heartbeat.

"You are beautiful," he murmured, kissing up her neck. "And you taste delicious." His lips were damp as he smiled down at her.

"Are you going to…do it now?"

"We should see if you're ready for me."

She frowned. "I don't know how."

"It's easy," he said. "Touch yourself between your legs."

"But…?"

"Just do it." He raised his eyebrows as though challenging her to disobey.

"Touch myself?"

"Ja."

She swallowed and ran her hands over her flat belly to the patch of hair at the juncture of her thighs.

"Lower," he said. "Touch your cunny, your entrance."

She parted her legs, just a little, and delved lower.

"What do you feel?" he asked.

"My-Myself."

"But not like usual, right?" He searched her eyes. "You're hot and wet and you have a hunger down there you didn't know you could experience."

She nodded.

"Tell me how wet you are?"

"That is a shocking question."

"It is one I need to know the answer to."

She smoothed through her soft folds, prodded her entrance. She was sopping, like nothing she'd known before. Her eyes widened and her breaths quickened. "I am very wet."

"Which tells me you want me," he said with a grin. "That you are ready for my cock."

"Oh, I don't know about—"

He was over her, between her legs, his weight held on his elbows. "We are man and wife. This *will* happen."

She stared up into his eyes. The depths glinted with longing.

"And I believe you are ready," he said.

"But how do you know, Ravn?"

"Because your cunny is wet. It is a gift from the goddess Freya so that a man's cock can glide into a woman's body and it be pleasurable for both parties."

"A gift from Freya?"

"*Ja.*" He dropped a kiss to her lips and his cock tip nudged her entrance.

She tensed.

"No, relax. You must relax."

"But I don't know if I can fit you inside me." She tensed and balled her hands into fists.

"You can. You will." He pushed forward a little more, gaining purchase.

"Ravn." She gripped his shoulders.

"Relax, give into it." He frowned. "And tell me when you have."

"I'm trying."

"Try harder."

She nodded and cupped his cheek. "I can do this."

"I know you can." He paused. "Are you ready?"

"Aye."

"So tell me what you want." There was a note of tension in his voice, as though holding back were suddenly taking a supreme effort.

"I want…"

"Say it."

"I want you. I want your cock inside me." And as she'd spoken, she'd realized it was what she wanted most in the world. To truly connect with her new husband—the only husband she would ever want or need. And it dawned on her: three years wouldn't be enough time with him.

Chapter Fourteen

R AVN STARED DOWN at Carmel's pretty face. Her cheeks were flushed a delicate pink and her were eyes wide with curiosity and need. "I won't hurt you," he said.

"I know," she whispered.

In the name of Odin, he hoped he could keep that promise. His cock ached with the need to drive deep and feel her wet pussy hugging his length. His balls were painfully tight with desire and he felt as though his blood were neat lust coursing through his veins.

He pushed forward into her tightness.

Her eyes widened and she hitched in a breath.

"It will feel so good," he managed, a tremble going down his spine. Holding back was agony of the most exquisite kind.

"I want you to do it."

"As I want to be inside you." He ducked his head and kissed her sweet lips, tasting her desire and adoring her all the more for trusting him with her delicate, virginal body.

When he felt her relax a little around his cock, he curled his hips and took her another inch.

She moaned, but her kiss intensified and that told him she hadn't hated his invasion. In fact, she'd enjoyed it.

A sudden, hot bluster of desire nearly had him plundering in, but he summoned willpower and started on a slow, gentle glide through her wetness. Her pussy fluttered around him and she canted her hips up to meet him.

A groan of longing rumbled from his chest. He reached downward, hooked his hand beneath her left thigh, and pulled her leg up to hug his hip. She opened up further and he rode deeper still.

"Ravn," she gasped against his lips. "Oh…"

"I'm nearly in and you feel so good, I could believe I'm already in Valhalla."

She moaned long and low.

He pushed in, to full depth, his balls pressing up against her. "Oh, fuck," he murmured, studying her closely. "That's it."

She clutched his shoulders. "You're in?" She gasped.

"*Ja*, I am inside you so fucking deep…so good."

He rolled his hips over her, catching her sweet, little bud with his body.

Her mouth formed a perfect '*o*' as she stared up at him with her breath trapped in her lungs.

"This is where the pleasure will start," he said, rolling over her again, not his entire weight, just enough to stimulate her. "Can you feel it?"

She nodded and drew up her other leg so she was clasping his hips with her knees. She let out a great exhale of breath.

"And there is no rush," he said, hoping his stamina was at full sail. "We have all night."

"Am I doing it right?" she asked.

"My love, you are perfect." He found her mouth and kissed her. With each stroke of his tongue, he ground onto her and drove deep.

Soon, their flesh was slick with sweat as they rode against each other and their breaths quickened.

His cock throbbed with longing. Never had he worked so hard to hold off. But this was special. Carmel was special. He wanted this to be perfect for her and that meant she had to climax this first time. Climax before him.

"Can you feel the wave of bliss coming?" he managed, his voice breathy and needy, even to his own ears.

"Aye…it's right there. It's like a storm inside me." She ran her hands down his back and clasped his ass cheeks, her fingernails digging in.

The action was nearly his undoing. To feel her touching him like that, needing him, wanting him, was almost too much to bear.

"Let it take you," he said, trembling as he held the majority of his weight above her. "Let it take you, feel it. I've got you. Fear nothing. I've got you."

"I'm going to…oh…oh…Ravn." She screwed up her eyes and pressed her head into the pillow. "Don't stop." The tendons in her neck strained and she gritted her teeth.

Then with an adorable squeal and a gasp, she pulsed beneath him and her back arched. Her pussy hugged his cock in a series of powerful waves. Ravn could contain himself no more and buried deep, allowing his seed to rush through his shaft. The moment of release was intense and perfect.

He buried his head in the warmth of her neck and let out a thick moan of pleasure. It seemed to go on and on. She matched him, taking him deeper, crushing against him as she pulled him closer.

"Oh, fuck," he gasped, closing his eyes. Bright lights flashed behind his lids and he had a sense of losing himself in her, becoming her. They were as one.

"Oh! Oh!" she cried, dragging her fingers up his back and gripping his shoulders. "Ravn…is that supposed to happen?"

"*Ja*, every second of it." He lifted his head. "It was good for you?"

"I have no…idea…what just happened to me." Her pussy was still gripping his cock in honeyed, little spasms and she was breathing in soft pants.

"You had the pleasure I was telling you about. That is the gift of the gods to a man and a women."

"It's…incredible and intense." She touched his cheek. "My body hardly felt like mine, yet at the same time, I felt more alive than ever before. It's like nothing I've ever known."

"I am glad you liked it."

"Ravn." She swallowed and stroked her fingers over his lips. "I more than *liked* it. When can we do it again?"

A laugh burst up from his chest. "Oh, devious Freya, what kind of nymph have you sent me for a wife?"

"I am not a nymph." She grinned. "Though right now, I do feel kind of fragile beneath you."

"Oh…right." He rolled off her, realizing some of his weight had slumped when he'd found his pleasure.

She curled up next to him, her warm, soft body touching his along the length of his side.

He pulled her closer, needing her in his arms. A rush of pride came over him. She might have been small and a long way from home, but she was brave and strong and full of determination. She was the perfect match for him and he'd do whatever it took to keep her safe and ensure she was happy in Drangar, so happy that she would want to stay forever and she'd forget about his promise to take her home in three years.

After a while, his eyes became heavy and his heart rate returned to normal. He gave in to sleep, feeling more content than he had in years.

A delicious warm blackness enveloped him and for once, he wasn't tormented by dreams of the past.

But then he woke, aware of her absence and of a cool patch at his side.

Instantly, he sat and looked around. All was quiet. The fire was still glowing and the heaviness of the dead of the night pressed down upon him.

Standing, he heard a noise from the bathing area. He took a few steps closer. Water splashed, the rustle of material, then the pull of a comb through hair.

Thanks be to Odin. She was perfectly fine and still here.

He went back to the bed, reached for a drink, then sat on the edge, waiting for her. A melancholy came over him. Regrets for things he'd done. He'd been spared those misdeeds in his dreams, but now they twisted around his mind and tugged at his soul.

After a few minutes, she appeared wrapped in a pale-gray fur. Light from the fire caressed her long, silken hair and the scent of lavender once again wrapped around him.

She stood before him and touched his chin. "You look sad, husband."

His throat tightened and he looked into her eyes.

"Did I do something wrong?" she asked.

"No. No, of course not." He reached for her and pulled her onto his lap. "You are utterly perfect."

"So why the downward tip of your lips?" She traced them with her fingertip.

He sighed. "I am a man with a past, a past I am not particularly proud of. And in turn, in the quiet of the night, like this, it makes me wonder if I even like myself."

She said nothing, waiting for him to go on.

"I took my first wife because I wanted sons, not because I loved her. She didn't deserve that. She was a kind, good, and loyal woman." He looked her straight in the eye, waiting for the disgust.

It didn't come. "Did you ever mistreat her?"

He shook his head. "No. She was always safe and fed and warm. I certainly never raised my hand to her. I provided and cared for her."

"And was she happy?"

He thought about it. "I think so."

"So there is no reason to berate yourself, Ravn."

For a moment, he was thoughtful, then, "And Haakon?" He traced the angle between her neck and shoulder that was peeking from the fur.

"What about Haakon?"

"You have met him. He is a fine Viking, with patience enough to tell sagas to children, anyone's children. He walked slowly with my father while I rushed to the sacred doors of

Uppsalla, and he didn't raid Tillicoulty. Instead, he has made it a better and safer place." He paused. "I cannot say that I would not have raided what I could have in his place."

"Would you now?"

He stared over her shoulder at an elk skull hanging on the wall. "They are good people there, families, like Drangar."

"So you would not?"

He didn't answer.

She ran her hand over his hair. "I think you are every bit as fine as your brother."

He huffed.

"What?"

"I tried to kill him." Again, he looked her in the eye. "I would have if my father hadn't stopped me. I was about to put a dagger through his heart."

"Why?" A muscle tensed in her jaw and she stiffened slightly.

"All in the name of power...which shames me." He swallowed tightly. "I stepped off the path of my destiny and behaved dishonorably. But the gods punished me for not believing in fate. A fate they had mapped for me when the stars were created." He hardly dared look at her face again. Carmel's opinion of him, he suddenly realized, was the most important one of all.

"But you have found your path now?"

"*Ja*, I have worked hard to find my path again. I flung myself at the mercy of Njord when I took to the ocean, and then I bestowed my brother with the respect his new crown deserves."

"And you regret your past mistakes?

"*Ja.*"

"God is merciful. God forgives."

"But do you?"

"I have nothing to forgive you for." She paused. "Unless you have only married me for the sons I will deliver."

He smiled, a slight tilt of his lips. "No, no, I have married you because you are the only woman I can imagine having at my side in this life and the next. I want you as my queen. It is your rightful place."

"I like that…even if it is for only three summers." She paused and raised her eyebrows. "That is what you promised, right?"

"I will make it so good, you will never want to leave." He tightened his hold on her. "Not in a thousand years."

"You will, huh?" She giggled and touched his cheek.

"I will be a changed man. My people will say it. Like a snake shedding its skin, I will be reborn."

"I have faith in you."

"You are brave to believe in me with such conviction." He swept his lips over hers. "And the gods smile upon brave women."

"I am also lucky, for what man other than you would have been so gentle with me on our wedding night, or as skilled?"

"'Skilled.'" He grinned, a lightness coming over him at the same time his cock stirred. "*Ja*, I am skilled."

She giggled as he tipped her to the bed, the fur around her torso falling away as he settled over her. Her laugh was such a delicate, sugary sound, his heart surged with love.

Love.

He was in love with his wife. So very much in love.

Catching her mouth in a deep kiss, he tried to show her how much she meant to him. How in awe he was of her. That he couldn't live without her. She made him a better man, and she would keep making him a better man.

Chapter Fifteen

THE KISS RAVN fed her was different. It was still full of passion, but also reverence and commitment. It was as though he never wanted to do anything other than lie with her, hold her, share his body with her.

She ran her hands over the warm expanse of flesh of his shoulders then traced the gutter of his spine.

He trembled beneath her touch and another surge of woman-power came over her. It was warm and settled in her belly. It flooded her veins and filled her heart. This big Viking warrior was as much under her command as she was his. They fit together despite their difference in size—despite her being in foreign lands and him being a powerful ruler.

"I am going to kiss you all over," he murmured against her lips. "And you will love it."

"I like you kissing me here." She reached for his face and pulled him in for another kiss.

He gave it, but after a moment pulled back. "I want to know every inch of your body with my mouth."

The grin he gave her was so sinfully devilish and full of wicked intent that her heart skipped a beat and her belly tightened. "But…"

"Shh, just relax and enjoy." His hair brushed her chin as he ducked to kiss the hollow of her throat and down her sternum.

She raised her arms and arched her back. It felt so right to be with him like this. Why had she dreaded it? She would do her best to relax into it.

The warmth of his lips spread to her left breast. He kissed the rise and then to her nipple. The hot, wet sensation of him taking it into her mouth again had her toes curling and her heart rate picking up. She felt his teeth and his tongue on her erect bud. It hardened further and she moaned and closed her eyes.

His big, hair-coated body over hers thrilled her and she pressed up to meet him.

He moved to her other breast and cupped her with his hand, still teasing her nipple with his thumb.

If he wanted to kiss her all over like this, she didn't mind.

After a few moments, he went lower, to her navel, his chest skimming over her thighs as he moved.

"Ravn." She rested her hands on his head. "I love your kisses."

He didn't reply but went lower, parting her thighs wide as he went.

"Oh." She lifted upward, her legs tensing, and rested her weight on her elbows. "What are… What are you doing?"

"I want to kiss you here." He set his lips over her pubic hair.

"But…" She squirmed. "I…"

"You what?"

"I… I bled, after…after…"

"After you lost your virginity?"

"Aye." She swallowed. There hadn't been much blood, just a few spots, and she'd washed herself clean.

"That does not matter to me," he said, running his hand from her ankle to her hip and back again as he smiled up at her. "You were a virgin on our wedding night. It is to be expected."

Before she could answer, he kissed her mound again, then pushed her legs wider, opening her pussy before him.

A tremble of self-consciousness besieged her. The room was lit softly with tallow candles, but still, to bare herself like this to a man, even her husband, was totally foreign.

"You are so pretty," he murmured, holding her a little firmer, as though sensing her need to squirm.

Her stomach clenched as he held her eye contact, then he poked out his tongue and licked over her sensitive bud.

She gasped and gripped the furs beneath her.

"Keep still," he murmured. "Trust me…again."

"But do you…?"

"*Ja*, I want to do this. I want to taste you, feel you come beneath my tongue. It is my greatest desire."

The lust dripping from his voice had her pussy clenching.

And then, as if he sensed that, he pushed one long finger into her.

"Oh!"

"Shh, enjoy. I know *I* will."

He closed his eyes and buried his face between her legs, the heated wetness of his tongue laving at her as he gently pumped in and out of her pussy.

She flopped back, one forearm over her eyes as she gave herself up to him. His technique was gentle yet still firm, and he seemed to know all the places inside and out that had pressure building in her pelvis.

His tongue worked her with enthusiasm, as though he wouldn't stop until she was gasping in delight. And that was when she felt it, the first spark of the pleasure she'd felt earlier when he'd taken her for the first time. It was deep in her womb and spread to her nub. It held the promise of a great wave of release that would result in toe-curling satisfaction.

She groaned and held him within the length of her legs and tilted her hips for more. All embarrassment left her as she concentrated on the building up of that delicious pressure.

He added another finger, gently stretching her, but it also seemed to touch a place inside her that was greedy for more.

"Oh… Oh, please… That's it. Just there…"

He upped the pace and rubbed her with more firmness.

Soon, she was gasping his name, crying out with the need to hit the high that would have her crashing into release. She thrashed beneath him, taking everything he was giving her.

It was there. The intensity so big, she couldn't contain it. Like before she held her breath for a few blissful moments then wailed as ecstasy rushed from her nub and her pussy. It pulsed through her body, filled her veins with boiling passion, and wetness gushed from her.

Her new husband stayed with her, extending the moment with his deft actions. She sprang forward, eyes open, and the sight of his head between her legs, moving in time with his tongue, had another wave of dark pleasure gripping her.

"Oh…oh…Ravn!" She clutched his shoulders and pulled him upward.

He raised his head and looked at her. He was grinning, his mouth and chin shiny with her moisture.

"Oh…that was surely…a terrible sin."

"No, my love, that was exactly how it should be. It is what the goddess Freya demands of her lovers. It is what every woman deserves from her man.

"It was… Oh…" She shook, a delicious tremble, and then she was in his arms as he seemed to hold her together. She sighed and melded into him.

He was breathing fast too, as though he'd been equally pleasured.

Resting her hand on his chest, she closed her eyes, her legs winding with his.

He dragged a fur over them and set his hand on her ass.

Outside, a dog barked and in the distance, an owl called.

They all seemed so far away. The entire village, Tillicoulty, her homeland—it was all so far away. Right now, there was only being in Ravn's arms, in this bed, in their house.

He kissed the side of her head. "Sleep. You must be exhausted."

"I am tired, but it is a happy tired." She paused and circled his left nipple. "A tired that is full of satisfaction, as though I have won in battle, or climbed a mountain, set my spear in the center of a target over and over."

"I'd say my spear hit target." He chuckled.

She looked up at him. "You say the most shocking things to a Christian woman."

He laughed. "I speak the truth."

She giggled and settled her head back down in the crook of his shoulder.

Soon, her thoughts were drifting and sleep encroached. An image of Thor's big, stone face filled her mind. It merged into a fluffy cloud shape with dark, stormy eyes and a cross for a mouth. Soon, it dispersed and was blown away and in its place, her dreams were filled with the ocean and forest, birds, fish, and the arms of her husband around her.

CARMEL SLEPT ON and on, a deep, restoring sleep that soothed away the weeks at sea and her nerves at lying with her husband. The warm, dark nothingness was a gentle healing balm.

When she woke, the light of the day pierced a few chinks in the wall with needles of sunshine. Haakon still slept at her side, his breathing steady and deep.

Gently, she stroked his chest, coiling her fingers in the hair there. It was thick and wiry and filled his sternum. He didn't stir and she swirled a little lower, into the dip, before the start of his strong abdominal muscles and where the hair thinned slightly. It then thickened just before his navel and she touched him here too.

"My love," he murmured, his grip on her tightening. "You are awake."

"As are you, King Ravn."

"This king slept as though dead." He chuckled softly. "You wore me out, sweet wife."

"I am glad you are not dead." She kissed his cheek. "I should hate that."

"Oh, no, right now, this moment, I am very much alive." He

flicked the fur that covered his legs and reached up to his belly. "And here is the proof."

She gasped. His dark cock was erect and jutting upward. The end was glossy and his slit a deep ruby red. The sight of his arousal so sudden and unexpected had her stomach tightening and a rush of anticipation gripped her.

He took his erection in his fist and stroked up to the tip, smoothing his thumb over the slit.

"You are so hard," she said.

"It is what happens when I wake beside a beautiful woman." He paused. "And all the harder when that woman is stroking my body."

She made a mental note of that and swirled the denser hair nearer to his cock. "Does that mean you want to fuck again?"

"I cannot imagine a time that I will not want to fuck you," he said, his voice gruffer than before. "But right now, I have another idea."

"You do?" She looked up at him, trying to read his expression. She could glean nothing.

"*Ja*, I wish you to return the favor."

"'Favor'?"

"*Ja*, take *me* in *your* mouth."

"Ravn...but...I..." Surely, she'd misheard him. What was he talking about?

"There is no *but*. I wish for your mouth to be around my cock, as though your mouth were your cunny."

"You want me to..." Her eyes widened at the very thought.

"Suck me, *ja*, fuck me with your sweet mouth and tighten your lips around me. Take me deep. No teeth, though. I'm not a fan."

"Ravn...that must..."

"Do not say it is a sin when it's pure bliss for a man."

"'Bliss'?"

"*Ja*." He squeezed her ass as he seemed so fond of doing. "Your mouth around my cock, warm and wet and adoring, will bring me such pleasure."

"I did not know."

"I have much to teach you." He grinned, that wicked, exciting tilt of his lips that did funny things to her insides.

She gulped and wondered briefly if her husband was the greatest sinner of all or if every man asked this of their wives. She pulled in a deep breath. "So you had better teach me this too."

"I am sure it will come naturally." He applied gentle pressure to her shoulder, as though urging her down his body the way he'd slid down hers the night before. "Do what feels right and you will soon know if it is."

She came face to face with his cock and he released it as though offering it to her to play with.

Play, aye, that is perhaps what I should do.

She took it in her hand and mimicked his previous movement, stroking it from root to tip.

He groaned and let his head flop back, his abdominal muscles tightened.

"You're hot," she said. "Your cock is hot."

"And you're making me hotter."

The bliss-soaked rumble in his tone gave her a smidgen of confidence and she held his cock still, poked out her tongue, and swept it over the tip.

"Ah, Carmel...*ja*...more." He rested his palm over her head. "More of your mouth."

His cock pulsed and the masculine scent of him filled her nose. Heat from his body poured onto hers and her pussy quivered with anticipation.

"Please."

Again, that sense of feminine power came over her. Ravn needed her in a real basic, primitive way right now and she felt ten times taller, a hundred times stronger for it.

But she would give him what he was practically begging for.

She opened her mouth and took the shiny, domed head of his cock between her lips.

He groaned, long and guttural. His body seemed to vibrate as though energy were battling to release.

Taking him a little deeper, his slightly salt flavor slid onto her tongue. She liked it—a lot—and wrapped her tongue around his thick shaft as if enfolding it in a blanket.

His fingers tightened in her hair and his thighs shook.

She guessed she was doing it right.

With her right hand, she caressed his leg, sweeping upward to his balls. Gently, she tickled over them with her fingernails.

"Oh, in the name of Odin," he muttered. "Carmel…"

That was his way of telling her he liked what she was doing. So she took him further into her mouth, until her cheeks puffed, and she cupped his balls so she could gently stroke over the sparser hairs at the base of them.

"Mmm…*ja*…fuck…" he moaned. "I like that."

She guessed he liked it a lot. So she pulled back, until his cock tip was sitting on her lips, then sank onto him again, feeding him into her mouth with her free hand.

His cock twitched and he lifted his hips slightly as if wanting to thrust into her.

"As though your mouth were your cunny."

His words came back to her, as did a memory of the night before. Him gently sliding in and out of her pussy in a steady rhythm. Was that what he wanted now? She didn't know, but she'd give it a go.

Bobbing up and down, she took him to the back of her throat and then almost released him, keeping her lips a tight band around his vein-rippled shaft.

Soon, he was moaning long and low. He drew up his legs and dug his heels into the furs. His hand on her head followed her movements and he gripped his other hand into a fist.

A slick of salt-laced liquid coated her tongue and spread its flavor. When he hit the back of her throat this time, she swallowed her saliva. The action tugged on the tip of his cock.

"Ah, fuck." He bucked his hips. "Carmel…"

He was close to spilling his seed, she knew that much. So she continued what she was doing. His balls receded into body and his cock stiffened to steel. He was gasping with each breath and his body as solid as rock beneath her.

"It's coming…" He panted. "Get ready… It's…coming."

He held his breath and she upped the pace using her hand on his slick cock as well as her mouth.

Then suddenly, a great wave of release filled her mouth. His cock throbbed as she swallowed.

He cried out in his own language, the deep bellow echoing around the room and up to the rafters.

Her pussy clenched and her heart skipped along in excitement. What had she just done? It had felt amazing—it still did—to feel him getting such pleasure from her.

Another release flooded her mouth. He thrashed beneath her for a few seconds, but then his hands were around her upper arms and he pulled her up his body so she was lying flush over his.

"Carmel." He was breathing fast as he pushed her hair over her ears and stared up into her eyes.

"Ravn."

"That was… You are…"

"I am a quick learner?"

For a moment. he said nothing, but then he nodded and laughed. "*Ja*. You are."

"So I did it right?"

"You do not even need to ask that question. You know the answer in your heart."

He pulled her down for a ravenous kiss and held her close, as though he'd never let her go and never want another.

Carmel had dreaded her wedding night all of her life. But in reality, it had been the opposite to the horrors in her imagination. There had been no pain, no humiliation, no battle of wills. Ravn had given her nothing but pleasure and beautiful memories.

She thanked God for her handsome, knowledgeable, and kind husband.

Chapter Sixteen

"WE WILL HAVE a festival," Ravn announced the next day in the village square.

"What kind?" Tyr the boatbuilder asked.

"A festival of skill, with weapons." Ravn pointed at the beach; the tide was on its way out. "We will find out who is the best shot with a bow and arrow, a spear, and a knife. The winner in each will win three gold coins and feast with myself and the queen at sundown."

"I will fire my arrow?" Thormod asked, slipping his hand into his father's.

"Not this time, son, but I will help you practice later." He stooped and picked Thormod up, settling him against his side. "Joseph, organize the targets, and Erin, ensure the feast will be spectacular for those who are triumphant."

"I'll throw a spear," Carmel said, tipping her head and studying her husband. At home, her father would have refused such a thing, despite her having the necessary skills. Women didn't compete with men; they were not as good, so what was the point?

"Excellent idea." Ravn grinned and wafted his hand in the air. "Shield-maidens and queens may also compete in our festival."

"And what is the festival to celebrate?" Erin asked.

"My beautiful, giving wife who has traveled land and sea to rule the good people of Drangar at my side." He cupped Carmel's cheek and set a kiss on her lips.

A cheer went up, the gathered crowd clearly enjoying their king's light mood and appreciating the reason why they were having a festival.

"Come," Tyr said to Joseph. "I will help with the targets."

The two men wandered off, gesturing as though planning on the construction.

"There are more people in Drangar who speak my language than I first knew," Carmel said to Ravn.

He slipped his hand around her waist and surveyed the horizon out on the fjord. "It is Joseph's doing. He might be Christian, but he is wise and he has told us that in order to trade with other lands we sail to, in order to conquer, we must speak a common language with those we meet."

"That is true."

"My father and his men sailed east a lot and learned the language of the people there. Many here still speak it. But Haakon and I were always more interested in sailing west."

"Why?" She picked up Thormod's small catapult that he'd dropped and passed it to him with a smile.

"We'd grown bored of the spoils of amber, furs, and autumn herring. We wanted more… We knew there was more."

"Gold crosses, brass candlesticks, silver coins." She raised her eyebrows.

"And beautiful women who know instinctively know how to please their husbands in bed."

"Shh." Her eyes widened and she nodded at Thormod.

Ravn laughed. "Do not fear. Viking boys learn about sex from a young age. He will take his first woman at thirteen; I will give her to him as a gift."

"What? But…"

"I will choose an older woman from the village, beautiful, *ja*, but older and experienced. It is as important as the day he gets his arm ring."

"Ravn, I really think that we…"

"You will not change all of my ways," Ravn said. "And I think you'll agree that the fact my father did that for me at thirteen pleases you very much. I was skilled last night, *ja*? It was not the blind leading the blind. I'd had a good teacher."

She stared into his flashing, blue eyes; the reflection of the fjord filled them. The image of her husband, at only thirteen, bedding an older village woman wasn't one she wanted in her head. "But Thormod should wait for the sanctity of marriage… I…"

"Marriage means many of the same things to us, but also some different." He kissed her again. "And I think you'll agree, so does being a woman here in Drangar." He raised his eyes knowingly.

Thormod pointed to the beach. "Look, Father. Look."

Tyr and Joseph were piling up two straw bales and beside them sat a large, round target, wooden and covered in white linen, with a red center.

The village men and women were gathering and three groups had partitioned themselves off. One held bows and arrows, another spears, and a final group clutched knives.

"Ah, good." Ravn set Thormod down. "We are nearly ready for our festival."

Carmel took the little boy's hand; she didn't want him running in front of a target if weapons were about to start flying through the air.

Along the pier, villagers lit fire baskets, and passed around horns of mead.

Carmel studied the villagers, laughing and talking, and the children and animals milling about. They seemed happy, content, and at peace with each other and their strange gods.

And right now, in this strange land, she felt safe. She felt cared for and respected. Helga even dropped a small, respectful bob as she walked past holding a tray of food. There was no jealousy or malice there, that much was clear.

And a relief.

Ravn had offered her a choice at three years, but at this moment in time, that didn't feel long enough. Carmel wanted these feelings for the rest of her life. Love. Serenity. Satisfaction.

But she wouldn't worry about the future now. Today was today…the present.

A few hours later, all was set and the people gathered.

"Let the tournament begin," Ravn bellowed as he raised his arms in the air.

The crowd hushed.

"As your king, your ruler, and a skilled warrior, I will be judge." He held out his hand to Joseph, who passed him a horn of mead. "And I wish you all the luck of the gods." He paused, then repeated the words in his own language.

A cheer went up.

"Archers, begin."

"I want to be archer," Thormod said, tugging on Carmel's gown.

"Do you?" She reached for him and he happily went into her arms and settled on her hip.

"*Ja.*" He took a lock of her hair and wound it around his finger, studying it. "Thormod archer."

"Then make sure to watch these skilled Vikings and see how they do it. Then when you are a big boy, you will be one of them."

"*Ja.* Thormod watch." He turned, his face serious and his eyes wide.

Carmel had the urge to kiss his soft, round cheek but resisted. She'd only just come into his life, but she hoped this would be the start of a close bond between them. He really was very sweet.

The first archer lined up his arrow and pulled it back in the string of his long bow. He was a tall, lean, young man with hair in a long plait. His tunic was blue and his pants and boots black. In his earlobe he wore a long golden chain that looped up to the top of his ear and pierced again.

He blew out a breath, seemed to steady himself, and then fired.

It hit the target, but not in the red.

"Ah, more practice for you, Bjorn. But you'll get there," Ravn called. "Next."

The second contestant was an older man, shorter, fatter, and with a thick, grizzly beard. He took aim, fired, and hit the target dead center.

"*Ja, ja*," Thormod said, bouncing in Carmel's arms.

The crowd cheered.

"Well done." Ravn nodded at him. "Next."

The final archer took his place, prepared, and fired. His shot was good but sat on the edge of the red.

"And the winner is Daneson," Ravn said, gesturing to the older Viking. "The queen and I look forward to feasting with you and your prize of three gold coins will be on your plate awaiting your arrival."

"I thank you." Daneson grinned.

"And onto the knives," Ravn said.

Carmel took a step backward as a huge Viking, minus his tunic, stepped onto the sand spinning a lethal tooth-edged knife in the air and catching it. She wouldn't like to meet him in battle, even with her best spear.

"Ah, we have my good friend Sindri," Ravn said, clasping him on the shoulder. "Let's see what you can do."

Sindri kind of growled and turned to the target. He gripped the handle of his knife as though still testing the weight of it, rocked back on his left heel, and then hurled it.

It flashed as it pierced the air and then slid almost silently into the center of the target.

The crowd roared, clearly impressed.

Sindri punched the air and beamed, showing a distinct lack of teeth.

Thormod clapped excitedly.

"He's good, right?" Ravn said to her. "Been at my side in many a battle."

"That sounds like the right side of him to be on," Carmel said.

Ravn chuckled then turned to watch the next knife thrower.

It was a woman and her blade was long and shone brightly, the handle made of bone. She didn't do any of Sindir's showmanship, simply stood in his footprints in the sand, took aim, and threw. Her knife spun once before landing on target.

Again, the crowd cheered.

She nodded once at them, then walked to her knife, snatched it up again, and re-sheathed it on her belt.

"Who is that?" Carmel asked Ravn.

"Bodil, Sindir's little sister. He taught her that. He'll be pissed now she's drawn level with him."

"If they both win, can they both dine with us?"

"Would you like that?"

"Aye, I'd enjoy the company of a shield-maiden, if that is what she is."

"Most definitely that is what Bodil is. She has been to almost as many battles as I."

"So she can dine with us?"

"If it would please the queen, then *ja*, she will dine with us." Ravn smiled then clapped as another knife thrower hit the target, but not the red, the white.

"And the joint winners are Sindri and Bodil. You will both feast with your king and queen this eve and receive three gold coins each." Ravn held up his hands as the crowd cheered and several slapped Sindri on his bare shoulders.

Bodil looked right at Carmel, her gaze unwavering.

Carmel held it, though she couldn't decide if it was hostile or curious.

She hoped for curious.

"Now for the spear throwing," Ravn said when the crowd quieted. "Who is to go first?"

"I will." A thick-shouldered man stepped forward with a thin fur draped over his tunic that was held in place with a large, brass brooch. He held a long, dark wooden spear with a highly polished pointed steel head.

He took his position farther back from the knife throwers, farther back from the archers too. The crowd cleared some room for him as he drew a line in the sand with the toe of his boot and then paced back some more.

He studied the target, littered with holes now, and hoisted his spear high, then he seemed to bounce on the spot twice before breaking into a run. After five paces, he hurtled the spear into the air.

It flew fast and straight before arcing down and hitting the white section of the target.

"Ah, so close," Ravn said shaking his head. "You'd have taken off the enemy's arm but not his head."

Thormod clapped, he was the only one; he must have been impressed with the show.

"Next," Ravn called.

Another man stepped up holding a long spear with a collection of feathers tied to the end. He wiped his hand over his hairless head—his scalp covered in ink—and took up the same position as the previous contestant. He blew out a breath and gritted his teeth, then with spear aloft, he took a run at his throw and launched the spear into the air.

Again, it flew in a graceful arc, the silver tip glinting in the sunshine.

Carmel felt her hair lift a little in the breeze and as it did so, the spear changed its trajectory very slightly. It hit with a solid *thud*, again on the white.

"Ah, bad luck, we have no winner for the spear," Ravn said.

"Hey, what about my turn?" Carmel set Thormod down on the sand.

"The line has been set a long way from the target, farther than I'd expected." Ravn turned to her.

"So? Let me try. I can throw a spear."

"But..." He appeared unsure now.

"I can throw a spear," she repeated. "And Queen Kenna's brother, Hamish, knows it."

Ravn stared at her for a moment and then turned to the crowd. "Get the queen a spear."

There were a few bemused looks and two dogs scampered over the sand chasing each other, but then a spear, slightly smaller than a man's, was offered forward by Bodil.

"Thank you." Carmel took it and nodded at her.

"I wish you the luck of the gods, Your Grace." She studied Carmel's eyes, as though fascinated by their green color, and then stepped away.

Carmel blew out a breath as the familiar weight of a spear settled in her hand. She passed it from one to the other, checking its straightness and examining the sharpness of the tip. It was not unlike the one she'd taken to battle in Tillicoulty and had never seen again. 'Haps this was the moment she reclaimed the part of her that had been on the losing side.

"Father," she muttered, "Guide me, I implore you." And she meant both fathers, God and King Athol.

"What is she doing?" Thormod asked Ravn.

"Your new mother is going to compete." Ravn picked his son up again. "Be quiet and watch."

Carmel concentrated on the target, letting the blood-red of the center imprint itself in her mind's eye. It was all she focused on. The villagers, the fjord, the jostling dogs all slipped away.

Then she took a few steps back, bouncing the spear before lifting it aloft. She blew out a breath, hoisted her gown with her free hand so that it was almost at her knees, and took four fast paces. She hurtled the spear into the vastness of the blue sky. It was slightly off on target, upwind, but on its downward trajectory, as it headed for the target, the breeze gave her what she'd bargained on. A slight huff, a trickle of air that just touched the sensitive spearhead and angled it straight toward the red center of the target.

It hit with a definite *thud*.

The crowd went wild. Punching the air, clapping, cheering. She'd done it. Now they'd seen the type of woman their new queen was.

"You are not just a pretty face," Ravn said, cupping her cheek and staring into her eyes.

"Did you ever think that's all I was?" She smiled up at him.

"No." He shook his head. "I always knew you were kind and strong, beautiful and loyal, but now I also know you are a skilled huntress. That pleases me."

"Ah, but what else don't you know about me?"

"That is what I intend to spend a lifetime finding out." He kissed her, a hard, deep, excited kiss that made her head spin.

When he pulled back, he raised her arm and turned her to the crowd. He shouted in his own language then repeated in hers. "Good people of Drangar, now you see what a talented queen we have."

The crowd cheered louder. Bodil was beaming and looking at Carmel afresh, respect in her eyes this time.

"How lucky we are that the gods saw fit to deliver me a woman who is a fine wife, lover, mother, and protector of our lands," Ravn called out. "Fate has been kind. We will give our thanks to Thor, Odin, and the goddess Freya for our good fortune."

Carmel felt like her heart would beat right out of her chest. Never in her life had she felt such warmth and adoration. With Ravn at her side, surely, she could achieve anything.

And with these people, the people of Drangar, she felt she really could be all the things Ravn had just said she was. Wife. Lover. Mother. Protector. Huntress.

Ravn spoke of his and his people's luck that she was there, but the truth was Carmel felt like God had truly shone his light upon her and blessed her with everything she'd ever wanted. She'd been seen and heard and her hope for the future was to deliver fine sons, but also daughters, because Drangar was a place for a girl to grow up knowing that there was no ceiling to her abilities. She could hitch her longboat to the stars if that was what she chose to do.

"I love you," Ravn said, kissing her cheek.

"And I love you, King Ravn of Drangar. I love you so much, and I always will."

His breath hitched and he held her tighter. "You do? You will?"

"Aye." She smiled. "And when you take me home in three years, I hope you'll stay a while, visit my family with me."

"And then… Then what? At the end of the visit."

"I do believe we will return to Drangar and our people." How had it happened so fast? She didn't know, didn't understand it. But this was her home now and she'd be content with visiting her family…on the understanding they accepted her choice of husband.

Would they?

Could they?

But that was a worry for another day. Right now, this day, everything was pretty much perfect.

Chapter Seventeen

TWO FULL MOONS later, the sun was filling the sky for many hours of the day, barely dipping below the horizon in the middle of the night.

The tiny bugs that plagued the summer months had returned and fires still burned in homes to keep them at bay. Ravn was bothered by them, but not as much as Carmel was. Her bites were sore and red and she kept covered up, her clothes scented with cloves.

"I am sorry for your discomfort," he told her, wrapping his arms around her small frame and pulling her back to his chest.

"It is not so bad." She set down her weaving shuttle. "The wee beasties were a pain in my homeland too."

"Would you like to leave Drangar for a while?"

"Where would we go?"

"To the coast. I have a small dwelling there. The insects do not breed in the open ocean, so it is much easier to live."

She turned within his arms. "It's true. It's still water they like and the forest is full of that."

"So? Would you like to take a trip away with me?"

She smiled and some of the tension left her shoulders.

Her smile filled his heart. Ravn knew he'd never been as in love as he was now, and each day, he fell for his wife a little bit more. She'd found her way into his soul. Without her, he'd be lost, a wanderer through life with a heart shredded.

"So is that smile a *ja*?" he asked, touching the tip of his nose to hers.

"Aye, I would like that, for a few weeks." She hesitated and he sensed there was something else she wanted to say.

"What, my love?"

"Just us?"

He tipped his head and a stir of interest heated his belly then traveled lower. "That was my plan."

"Mmm."

"Do you want company? Erin? Bodil?"

"No, no, not at all. I only want to be with you. It will be nice."

"More than nice." He tugged her closer, his cock stirring at the feel of her soft body.

"But…"

"'But'?" He raised his eyebrows.

"I do have a request."

"Whatever you want it is yours. All you must do is tell me." And he meant it. He'd give her the world if he could and all the gold and silver in it. He only wanted her to be happy and have everything she needed. He'd spend the rest of his life making up for the fact his brother had treated her as a slave.

"I would like"—she touched his lips—"to only speak your language while we are there."

"But…why?"

"I am Queen of Drangar, am I not?"

"*Ja*, you are."

"Then I need to be able to speak to all my people in their tongue. I feel a fraud that I cannot when so many speak mine."

"You are not a fraud," he said firmly. "You are married to the king, which makes you queen."

She nodded. "Exactly, and how can I hear their grievances, listen to their joy, converse with them if I cannot speak Viking?"

"You are right. You should have that knowledge."

"Good, so we are agreed. We will go to the coast, just the

two of us, and when we return. I will know the language of my new people."

"That is a trade." He ran his hand down her neck, over her right breast, and then rested it on her flat belly. "Maybe you will also return with an heir inside you."

"That would be a blessing from God, indeed."

"I will make offerings to Odin and all the gods before we journey."

"What about Thormod? Will he come with us?"

"Not on this occasion. I will ask Helga to care for him. 'Haps when he has a sibling, we will take them both."

"If that's what you wish."

"It is." He dipped his head and kissed his beautiful wife. Her lips were as soft as petals and she tasted sweet like honey. He intended to make the most of their privacy on the coast and indulge his near-constant desire to be inside her. What could be a better way to spend the summer?

TWO DAYS LATER, Ravn mounted his favorite horse, which had been packed up with supplies.

Carmel sat on a gray mare and with a look of excited anticipation. He'd made the right decision to take her away from the stuffy, busy town of Drangar for a while.

He'd left instructions with his three councilors to oversee the harvest and repair some defenses just outside of the town boundary. He'd sent an envoy south to get news from the next kingdom and a group of men had taken a boat east in search of amber and furs and possibly slaves.

"*Er du klar?*" he asked.

"What does that mean?"

"Are you ready?"

"Aye, I am," she answered.

"*Ja, jeg er.*"

"What does that mean?" A slight frown creased her brow.

"It means 'Yes, I am.'"

She repeated it with concentration.

"And so the lessons begin," he said with a smile as he kicked his horse on. "When we return, you will be thinking in my language."

"I hope so."

They rode out of the village amongst several shouts of *good luck* and *safe journey*. Ravn nodded seriously, though Carmel smiled and waved and called her thanks.

Her light nature and ready smile were just a couple of the things he loved about her. She softened his sharp edges and was an ointment to his sometimes-fractious mood. It was as though Freya had known he'd need someone with the opposite temperament to his but at the same time someone who was still strong and skilled and regal.

Ja, she was perfect.

The journey to the coastal spot Ravn had in mind was a half-day's ride through the forest and then another few hours past the steep entrance to the fjord.

As soon as they came out of the forest, the air was crisper and laced with the tang of salt. His stomach tightened with a sudden longing to be at sea. Sailing was in his blood. Exploring was his destiny.

Even though I've found what I was looking for?

He glanced at Carmel, who was studying the majestic cliffs with a look of awe in her eyes. Her skin was so delicate, her neck slender, and her hair flowing behind her, catching on the breeze. He knew the strands felt like silk when they lay on his naked chest or better still were spread on his abdomen.

The need to jump onto a longboat and hit the open ocean suddenly dissipated. He didn't want to be anywhere except right where he was, at his wife's side.

"The cliffs are beautiful but useless for crops," she commented.

"They are made from the body of Ymir. His bones had to go somewhere."

"Ymir?"

"*Ja*, it is how the gods created the world. From Ymir's blood, they made all the sea and the lakes. They used his flesh to create the earth we stand upon. And his hair, they made the trees and all their leaves and branches." He pointed upward. "And from his bones, the mountains were shaped. They made rocks and pebbles from his teeth and jaws."

"Bones." She frowned at the rocks. "But—"

"I know it is not your belief, but it is mine."

"And I respect that." She paused. "It is also quite a fascinating concept."

"It makes sense." He shrugged.

"Though if the sea and lakes are his blood, would they not be red?"

"They were once. They have been diluted now."

She nodded and her attention went to the horizon. The ocean had come into view, thickly blue and sparkling. "There is also a story in the Bible about the rivers turning to blood."

"There is?"

"Aye, when God was angry, he turned the Nile to blood. The fish died. The river was smelly and couldn't be drunk."

"Your god was indeed angry to do such a thing."

"I am glad not to see it."

"Ah, but I'd wager you are glad to see that." He pointed forward.

In the distance, against a strip of sand and sheltered by a tall, sheer rock was a small dwelling, a pit house. He'd made it many years ago with Haakon and Orm. They'd been young and keen to show they were capable of building a robust shelter.

"Oh…is that where we're staying?"

"*Ja*. You will like it. The air is fresh and clear, the fish plenti-ful, and there are scallops, crayfish, and mussels, more than we could ever eat."

"You make my stomach rumble." She laughed.

"We will be happy there." He kicked his horse on, keen to get there now that it was in sight.

The home was a quarter buried. They'd dug deep into the peat so that the door was several steps down. This had made it easy to construct half stone, half wooden walls, and a roof of two large, flat panels that reached a peak in the middle. The roof was covered in soil and grass and they'd decorated the highest point with replicas of Thor's hammers. There were no windows, but a hole to let smoke out in the rear gave enough light inside. Mainly, it was a summer dwelling, used for sleeping and storage when hunting and foraging in the area. The circle of thick stones outside was used as a seating area and sat around another fire pit with supports for a cauldron. It had been two years since he'd visited, but he hoped it was still stocked with wood and the roped bed frame was still intact.

"Already, the wee beasties are dispersing." Carmel smiled and pushed up the sleeves on her tunic. "What a relief."

"There are none at the house," he said. "You will be quite safe naked."

She laughed. "Safe. Naked. With you around, husband? I think not."

"Ah, 'haps you are right. You might be safe from biting insects, but not from a horny king who simply can't get enough of you."

She laughed.

Soon, they dismounted on a patch of bright-green grass that had a stream running at its edge and left their horses to graze.

Before long, they'd unpacked and Ravn had a fire going.

"We do not need to hunt or fish tonight," Carmel said. "We have supplies."

"That is good." He stood and shucked off his tunic, the sun instantly warming his skin. "For I have the bed to attend to."

"It could do fresh straw in the mattress." She pinched her nose. "It smells as though a wanderer wintered here."

"I will do that now."

"And I will bathe, in the stream."

He nodded and ducked inside, keen to get the bed to his wife's liking. Otherwise, she wouldn't be lying with him on it and he was counting on that.

It didn't take long to burn the straw that was in it and fill it with fresh. He then strapped it down with blankets and furs and a feather pillow he'd brought and knew she liked. Quickly, he lit the fire in the pit house to rid it of any small creatures and bugs.

He went outside.

And stopped in his tracks.

If he thought the gods had blessed him with a perfect woman, now he knew they truly favored him. More than that, he'd been absolved from his previous crimes and corruptions. That had to be the case. Why else would they have sent this woman, this goddess to him?

She was naked in the stream beside a small fall of water over round, rusty-brown rocks. It bubbled and frothed around her upper thighs and right now, as he watched her, she had her head tipped to the sky, her long, wet hair flowing down her back and her pert breasts jutting upward.

His cock went from soft to hard in about three heartbeats.

"Freya, I will make offerings to you every day from now until my last for your generosity."

He stepped forward, undoing his belt as he went. It fell to the ground behind him. He hopped on one foot, removed a boot, then the other. By the time he'd reached the shallow bank, he was naked and his blood ran on pure lust.

She turned and bent to reach the soap she'd left on a rock. Her ass stuck into the air now and her hair fell forward. He could just see the lips of her pussy, soft and inviting and all his.

Ravn didn't even notice the mountain chill of the water as he waded in and it did nothing to dampen his arousal. "My love," he said, pacing up behind her and clasping her waist. "You are a selkie, a siren, a sea nymph, 'haps all three."

She gasped and went to turn, but he kept her tipped over the rock before him and stared at her pale, round ass.

"Like this," he said, angling his erection at her entrance. "I am going to take you like this now. I have waited long enough."

"Ravn," she gasped, her voice laced with her longing—a sound he knew well now.

"You tempt me so by bending over in the water, naked, that I feel I have no control over my body. It needs you. *I* need you." He pushed into her warm wetness, a direct contrast to the cool water. "Oh, in the name of Odin. *Ja...*"

She reached around and gripped his thigh as though to keep him there. "Ravn...aye, more..."

"You will get more." He kept on going, his way eased by her arousal. When he reached full depth, her sweet body tight around his, he raised his face to Valhalla and let out a long, deep groan. It was a perfect moment of bliss and contentment and it was all wrapped up in a need to climax and hear her cry out in ecstasy.

He began to fuck her, each swing of his hips taking him deep inside her. He was breathing fast, and so was she. The water sloshed around them, the noise of the shallow falls at his side competing with the pulse in his ears.

Her pussy gripped him and he knew she was getting close. Each time his cock tip rubbed over her sweet spot, she let out a throaty grunt and her fingernails dug into his thigh.

His balls ached and his abdomen was tight with the need to come. "Oh...fuck..." he managed, desperate to wait until Carmel had orgasmed. "Are you...?"

"Aye...aye..." She released his thigh and placed her hand between her thighs. The shifting of her arm told him she was working her nub.

To see that in and of itself was so hot, it nearly had him releasing.

He bit on his bottom lip and closed his eyes. Fucked her harder, dragging her onto his cock as he thrust forward.

"Oh!" She cried out. "Ravn!" Her yell was high-pitched and

sang into the woodland. Several birds took to the sky shrieking.

And then she held her breath, her pussy clamped around him for a few delicious seconds and then she was cumming around him. Squeeze and release, a gush of moisture, and her body was shaking and writhing, twisting and bucking back for more.

With a huge sense of relief, he allowed his own climax to claim him and in a rush of pleasure, he filled her with his seed, burying deep, claiming her as his own with each pulse of his orgasm.

"That is… That…" He could hardly string words together, the pleasure was so intense. She'd offered herself to him like this on their wedding night. He'd declined, but oh, it had been worth the wait.

She hung her head and stilled.

He ran his fingertips from the gutter of her buttocks up her spine and brushed her hair from her nape so it hung over her right shoulder. "Did you enjoy that?"

"You know I did." She was breathless. "It's so…so deep."

"Maybe we have just made our son."

"I feel like we might have." She pushed forward and his cock slipped from her pussy.

"My love." He reached for her and pulled her close. Her nipples were hard, little pebbles against his bare chest. "*Vi skal knulle hele dagen og hele natten mens vi er her.*"

"And that means?" She touched his cheek and smiled.

"'We are going to fuck all day and all night while we are here.'"

"Suits me." She reached up and kissed him. "That really, really suits me."

As her tongue tangled with his, a new heat rushed to his cock and he knew he'd be hard again within minutes. His new wife was too tempting and he had no intention of resisting.

Chapter Eighteen

CARMEL LAY CURLED against her husband in the small pit house he'd made so welcoming. But she couldn't get warm despite the fact that her skin was hot.

The fire had dwindled and she turned to the embers onto a cool patch of the bed. A full body shiver attacked her; it went from her toes up her spine and almost rattled her teeth.

She moaned quietly and became aware of her temple throbbing, as though the beat of her pulse were trying to get out. She swallowed, her throat scratched and thick, as though it had clogged up with spiky moss.

She sat on the side of the bed. Her head spun and she swallowed again. Her throat was so sore and dry. She needed fluid.

Standing, she reached for the table, but disoriented all of a sudden, she bumped into a storage box and then lunged forward. "Oh!" Her shins hit something hard and unyielding, sending shooting pains through the bones. Her body doubled over something solid and her ribs screamed a complaint. Then as she hit the earth floor, her wrist took the impact.

"Carmel!"

Ravn was at her side, reaching for her, his arms beneath her scooping her up.

"What is the matter?" he asked, going back to her language despite the fact that for one week, they'd only spoken his.

"I... I don't know..." She curled her fingers around her throat. "It hurts. I hurt."

"Let's get you back on the bed."

Seemingly without effort, he laid her on the bed, her head sinking into the pillow. "I'll get you a drink."

Within seconds, a mug of fresh stream water was at her lips. She sipped then winced when it felt as though there was thorns in it.

"You are burning up," he said, resting the back of his hand on her forehead. "You are sick."

"I know." She looked up into his worried eyes. "I feel... I feel..."

"Rest. Do not speak. I will care for you."

She could hear the anxiety in his tone. He was no medicine woman and they were not in the village, where he could have quickly gotten help.

"I'll be well by morn," she said, managing to smile weakly.

"I will pray to the gods that you are." He took her wrist in his hand. "This is bruising. I will make a paste to put on this."

"And my..." She paused and shivered uncontrollably. "My legs, my... I banged the box." Her shins were throbbing, adding insult to injury.

He lifted the blanket and frowned. "They are bruising already. You should have woken me."

"I just wanted a drink..."

"Here, have some more. My mother always said when the sweats come, you need to drink to replace the water dripping from your skin."

She sipped some more, then a feeling of absolute exhaustion came over her and she melted into the pillow, eyes closing, blackness coming over her.

RAVN COULD FEEL his soul twisting as though it were being made into a rope and pulled long and taut. He set the mug aside and stared at his pale, sleeping wife.

She'd been perfectly fine all day. They'd fucked as soon as they'd woken, then together, they'd collected shellfish and cooked them with fresh garlic and herbs. She'd repaired some linen blankets and he'd made arrowheads ready for hunting, then he'd brought her to climax with his tongue when the sun had dipped and they'd sat around the fire.

Yet now she lay with the sweats, her voice croaking, her wrist and shins bruised and swollen, and her skin as white as lily of the valley.

Dread took hold. A gripping fist around his heart.

He'd seen this before in the village. A swift, brutal illness that took loved ones from families between dawn and dusk.

"Please, no. Let her be well. All Father, I beg you." He leaned forward and kissed her clammy forehead then dashed from the pit house. The plants he needed were by the copse of trees near the stream. Quickly, he paced past the horses, who raised their heads to watch him, then he splashed through the water and stooped to snag up the cropleek. When he had a fistful, he grabbed garlic and wormwood, enough to make a tincture.

That would help the bruising, but what about her sweats and obvious pain in her throat?

As he rushed back, he had a sudden longing for his sister. Astrid would have known what to do. She was good at staying calm in a crisis and thinking straight—and her thoughts were full of herbs and medicines, runes and what offerings to make to the gods.

But she wasn't here. She wasn't with him. And until a few minutes ago, Ravn had been the happiest he'd ever had been. Being all alone with his wife in their own little paradise had made his soul sing. But now…now he wished for his family, his sister and brothers, his parents, to help him heal the most important woman in his life.

I can't live without her.

His heart squeezed with each beat as he checked on Carmel

again then set to work on the tincture. Once it was a smooth, green paste that smelled both garlicky and earthy, he carefully rubbed it on her shins and wrist before bandaging over the balm to keep it in place.

"Freya, protect my love, my one true love, I beg you." He touched the cross at Carmel's ear. "And if you are listening, Carmel's god, please heal your faithful follower. She is everything to me and you do not need her in your heaven yet. She has things to do here. Children to bear, a people to rule, and a thousand more smiles to enjoy."

His breath caught in his throat and he realized it was a sob. Ravn hated crying, yet the pain of it in his chest was almost his undoing.

He gripped his wife's hand and knelt on the floor at her side, kissing her knuckles, and kept his attention firmly on the rise and fall of her chest.

She couldn't die.

She just couldn't.

They'd spent their whole lives looking for each other. Traveled over land and sea to be together. This couldn't be the end when it was barely the beginning.

Ravn just wouldn't let it be.

He tipped the water mug to her lips again and she stirred. With her eyes closed, she took a sip. She winced as she swallowed.

"Good. You must drink, even though it pains you," he whispered as he touched her forehead again.

The heat of her skin was like the ironsmith's furnace.

He pulled at the blanket, exposing her breasts. Sweat shone on her sternum, even though her skin goose pimpled.

"No..." she moaned.

"We must cool this fever," he said, reaching for a square of cloth and then soaking it with water. "Here, this will help."

Very gently, he wiped her forehead then each of her cheeks.

She murmured but didn't stop him.

He washed her neck, carefully pushing strands of damp hair aside. Then he re-soaked the cloth and carefully cooled her sweet, little breasts, tenderly calming her hot skin over and over.

She sighed and seemed to settle into the treatment. After a while, she fell asleep again.

He left her uncovered and collected fresh water. He found some loganberries and rinsed them should she want food when she woke.

On and on, she slept.

Ravn couldn't eat himself. Fear knotted his guts. It didn't feel like there was room for even one nut.

He paced around the pit house. He collected logs. He walked to the beach and looked out at the horizon. But every few minutes, he checked on his wife. Her sleep was deep and still and at one point, he worried that her breathing had stopped. He'd tipped his head over her face praying for the faintness of warm air on his cheek. There was. What a relief.

The sun lifted to the highest point then arced back toward the mountain. Ravn set to work on a chair, banging big pieces of smooth wood together. Perhaps when Carmel got better, because she would, he'd make sure of it, she'd like to sit and watch the ocean from it.

He paused, hammer aloft. A noise. From inside the pit house.

"Carmel." He dropped the hammer to the ground with a *thump* and rushed inside.

She was sitting, blanket fallen to her waist, and was reaching for the water.

"Here, let me." He was quick to reach it. "It's fresh."

She grimaced and nodded.

"Your throat is still dry?"

Again, she nodded and took the drink from him. This time, she took several big gulps.

"That's good," he said. "Are you feeling a little better?"

"My throat," she said in a croaky voice as she circled her neck with her palm.

"Let me see." Quickly, he lit a candle and held it by her face. "Open up."

She did as he'd asked.

"Oh, that's not good." He shook his head. "You look like you've had a swarm of bees in there. It's red and swollen and dotted with yellow stings."

"It happened once before," she said. "Like this." She took another drink.

"It did?" And she'd lived to tell the tale. Relief flooded him. It was a welcome change from the fear he'd been carrying around all day like a huge sack of sand on his shoulders.

"Aye, it came from nowhere. My mother nursed me."

"What did she give you?"

"Water with a wee bit of salt to wash my throat out and spit, and then hot water with honey to drink."

"I can do that." He gripped her hand. "And do you think that will heal you?" He could hardly say the next words. "Stop you from dying?"

She smiled weakly and touched his cheek. "I will not die. The fever has broken. It is just my throat that needs to heal—and it will."

"You scared me so." He kissed the center of her palm. "It came on so sudden. I thought… I thought…"

"Please." Her eyes were soft. "If you could get what I need."

"Of course." He jumped up. "We have honey in our supplies, and I will boil water and get the salt too."

Ravn raked through the box and found the honey, then hurried outside to put water over the fire. A sense of purpose was a much more welcome friend than fear and helplessness.

Carmel spent the next cycle of the sun sleeping on and off. When she woke, she gargled with saltwater and sipped honeyed water. Ravn hovered over her, quick to get anything she needed, quick to check on her as she slept.

He finished the chair. It was big and wide and he covered it in soft blankets and throws so it would be comfortable for Carmel.

Day barely turned to night once again, but the birds roosted for a few hours and a pink-and-lilac hue claimed the eastern sky. Ravn lay beside his wife and slept on and off, constantly aware of her breathing and dreading the fever returning to her soft, delicate skin.

At one point, he heard what he thought was an elk passing by. The crushing hooves on foliage gave it a way. Again, he thought of Astrid. She had a runestone she called "Algiz" and had said it represented an elk. When he'd once asked what that meant, she'd told him that it was a strong, protective rune that shielded a vulnerable person against evil with its mighty antlers.

And so right now, he was glad of the elk. His wife needed all the protection from evil she could get. Her disease had been swift, dark, and incapacitating. The elk passing by was a good omen, he was sure of that.

A little while later, he rose and bathed in the cool stream. He finally managed to eat some fish and berries, and then he prepared a little porridge for Carmel. That would be soft for her to swallow, and she did need to eat today. She was small enough. He didn't want her to lose weight.

She was stirring when he went back into the pit house and he kissed her forehead, glad to find it still cool.

"Here." He passed her water.

She took it, imbibing several mouthfuls before speaking. "Thanks." Her voice wasn't as croaky.

"How are you feeling?"

"Better. My throat is still a wee bit sharp, but I'm better than I was. Before, my head was spinning and banging like a drum and I kept thinking there were tiny dragons breathing fire on me, all over."

"'Tiny dragons'?"

"Aye…" She smiled. "I guess my dreams were playing tricks."

"Your skin was hot."

"But not because of dragons, right?"

"No, not because of dragons."

She sat completely upright. "Can I have my tunic?"

"Of course." He helped her put it on. "And I've made you porridge."

"That's kind of you."

He huffed. "It is not kind—it's necessary. You must eat."

"Well, I thank you for caring."

"I care more than you will ever know." He passed her the food. "I will chop logs while you eat. Then I have a surprise for you."

"'A surprise'?"

"*Ja*. But eat up first."

Chapter Nineteen

C ARMEL ATE MOST of the porridge. It scraped on her throat, but her stomach demanded feeding. Her mind went back to the previous episode she'd had like this. Her mother had fussed and fret, as had her father, but she'd bounced back in a few days and had almost forgotten all about it.

Until now when it had come again.

Thank goodness once more her body had fought the sickness.

After using the pail of water to freshen up, she wrapped her hands around the warm mug full of honeyed water and stepped outside into the bright daylight.

The scents of outdoors filled her nose and she breathed deep, enjoying the earthy, grassy, briny smells that were laced with salt. It was good not to have her head throbbing, though her shins and wrist ached. Ravn must have put the bandages on them. She couldn't remember doing it herself.

"Hey, what is that?" She pointed at a big pine chair covered in soft furs.

Ravn looked up, axe in hand. "You like it?"

"Aye, I do."

"I thought you might like to recover in comfort with a view, so I made it."

"You're very thoughtful." She walked up to it and ran her fingertip over the smooth back.

"You're still so pale." He was in front of her. A few dots of perspiration sat on his brow and his torso was bare, showing his dark chest hair and where the sun had licked his shoulders.

"I do feel tired," she confessed. "But I've had enough of lying in the dark."

"Of course. That's why I made this." He sat heavily in it then reached for her.

The next thing Carmel knew, she was on his lap and his arms were around her. He pulled a fur over her legs and cuddled her close.

"Drink your honey," he said, pressing a kiss to her temple.

She took a sip.

He stroked her hair, his touch tender. After a few minutes, he spoke. "I don't know what I would have done if I'd lost you."

"You lost a wife before and you survived."

He frowned. "That is true. But…"

"'But'?"

"But with you, it is different. I feel that we were destined, that the gods set us on a long path to find each other and then be together. I couldn't have stood it if we'd walked that path for so little time."

"I am almost better." She touched his cheek. He had a thick fuzz of dark stubble.

"I thank the gods for that." He tipped his head back, gesturing behind himself. "If you had been taken from me, I would have forsaken my crown, my life would have been over, and I would have come to live here with nothing but my memories."

"My love, but you are a king."

"I would not wish it any longer."

"So you would become a hermit? Here?"

"*Ja*."

"Without a wife, you would grow a great, shaggy beard. You would wear unkempt clothes and have long, unsightly toenails."

He chuckled. "And a handsome sight I would be."

"I think not." She shook her head. "And it would make me sad, looking down from heaven to think that was what you'd become."

"So, my dearest, beautiful wife." He nipped her chin. "Do not die on me. For now you know my dismal fate if you do."

"I will try my best"—she swept her lips over his—"to stay alive."

He held her tighter.

Carmel adored the way her husband made her feel so cared for. As though she truly was the only woman he saw. She hoped she'd give him many sons and that they'd have a long and happy life together.

"Here, let me take that." He set her empty mug aside.

"Thank you."

"And rest. You need to regain your strength."

"Do you have chores?" she asked.

"*Ja*, this. My job is to hold you safe and warm."

She sighed, settled her head against him, and looked out to sea.

It was a calm day. The waves whispered onto the sand and the water reflected the blue of the sky. The sun shone bright and white, a brilliant, diamond orb, and to her right, the horses grazed and swished their tails.

A sense of contentment filled her. God's beautiful creations were awe-inspiring and the love in her heart for Ravn over-flowed, filling her with warmth.

He drew a gentle circle on her arm and his breathing slowed.

She guessed he'd had a broken night worrying about her. He could do with sleep too.

A warbler set up its familiar chirpy song in the reeds and she let her thoughts drift as she watched the constant movement of the ocean.

She was just starting to fall asleep when she spotted some-thing on the horizon. Shielding her eyes, she peered forward. Was it what she thought it was?

"Ravn. Look."

"Mmm?"

"Out there. It's a... It's a longboat."

"What?" He tensed.

Red sails billowed and tall prow carved through the water. The hull was lined with shields and the oars left specks of white on the blue surface.

"Can you see a banner?" he asked.

"I'm not sure?" She unwound from her husband's arms and stood.

Ravn hopped up and for a moment disappeared. When he returned, he wore his belt with axe, dagger and sword attached. He also held a shield. His expression had gone from relaxed to grim.

He stomped to the rise of the beach that led down to the waves.

"I think I can see something," she called. "A banner."

"What color?"

"Black with red on it."

"That is the banner of... In the name of Odin... I can't remember, but I've seen it... I..."

"It is the banner of Tillicoulty."

"What?" He spun to her. "This longboat has come from the new home of my brothers and sister?"

"I believe so. And I can see it clearer now. Aye. It has a horse hoof and a fish on it."

"Do you think they can see us?" He rubbed his temple and frowned, as though emotions and thoughts were colliding in his mind.

"Light the fire." She stooped for firewood.

"No. Not you. Sit down. You have to rest. I will do it."

"But I can help. I am—"

"I was not asking. I was telling you, Carmel. You're what is important here, not this longboat." He threw fresh driftwood on the dwindling fire. It caught almost immediately. "No matter who is on it."

Carmel sat on the smooth furs, glad to take the weight off her weak legs. She quickly removed the dry bandages on her wrist and shins and tied the laces of her boots, which she'd left undone when coming out of the pit house.

"They're turning this way," Ravn said, waving.

"You're sure they are friendly?" she asked, wondering where her own dagger was.

"We are on good terms with Tillicoulty, are we not?"

"Aye." Unless King Haakon had decided to add to his collection of crowns and come to claim Drangar.

Ravn didn't seem to think of this and grabbed a torch, holding it aloft with flames and smoke licking the sky as he went down to the water's edge.

There was no pier, nowhere for the boat to dock.

"Brother!" A deep voice carried on the sea breeze.

"Orm? Is that you?"

"*Ja*. It is me! Your favorite sibling returned."

She peered forward. It was definitely Orm. She recognized his tall, lean body and long, dark hair.

Orm then dragged at his tunic, pulled it off, and stepped high on the prow. In one smooth dive he entered the water with barely a splash.

He swam like a seal, slick and fast, and within a minute was striding out of the water, pushing his hair back from his kohl-streaked face. Water clung to his trousers and dripped down his bare torso.

Ravn rushed to meet him.

"Why are you here?" Ravn asked, embracing his brother. "It is good to see you."

"That is unexpected welcome." Orm slapped Ravn on the shoulder and raised his eyebrows.

"I am in a good mood." Ravn laughed.

"And not in your kingdom." Orm looked around with his arm draped over Ravn's shoulder. "We haven't been here for years."

"Carmel wished some sea air." Ravn gestured to Carmel.

Orm appeared to notice her for the first time. He walked

closer, the sun sparkling off his wet skin. "Carmel? Your thrall, brother? Our prisoner?"

"*Ja.* Carmel."

"Orm," Carmel said, not getting up and giving him a curt nod.

"Well, it is good to see you too." Orm rubbed his hands together and grinned. "Because you can get to work and prepare my brother, the king, and me a drink to celebrate being reunited in our homeland."

"I don't think so." Ravn scowled.

Carmel held her hand up. When she spoke, it was in Orm's own tongue. "I am pleased you have had a safe journey, brother-by-law, but you will address me as 'Your Grace' from this moment on. And it is *you* who will fetch the mead from the pit house."

Orm's mouth hung open and he rubbed his eyes. He stared at Carmel then turned to his brother. "What is she saying?"

"You heard," Ravn said, stepping up to Carmel and taking her hand. He kissed her knuckles. "Carmel is my wife, which makes her Queen of Drangar. You will address her appropriately if you and I are to remain friends."

"You married the slave?" Orm's eyes were wide as he shook his head. "And I thought you took her to protect Tillicoulty and—"

"It doesn't matter what you thought, Orm, because you forgot one important point. Carmel is a princess by birth. She has royal blood and is a fine leader, huntress, and councilor at my side in Drangar."

"But she is a prisoner, a thrall, and a Christian at that. She cannot rule Drangar. It is not—"

His words were cut short as Ravn drew his blade and angled it at Orm. The tip was dangerously close to the dip of his throat. "The way you speak is treason. Be careful, brother. Be very careful."

Orm stepped back, sighed, then turned and kicked a stone down to the shoreline. As it splashed into the fizz of the waves, his frustration seemed to go with it. He turned with a grin. "To the King and Queen of Drangar." He held up his hand as though raising a horn of mead.

Ravn exhaled and re-sheathed his sword. He held Carmel's eye contact for a moment.

She smiled at him, glad to see the tension slipping from his shoulders. Orm wasn't her favorite person in the world, not by a long shot, but as a good Christian, she would practice tolerance and maybe even forgiveness for the sake of her husband.

"Who is on the boat with you?" she asked Orm as he helped himself to a handful of nuts from a bowl.

"A small crew. And…" He waggled his eyebrows. "My wife."

"Your wife?" Ravn spun to look out at the figures on the boat.

"Anna?" Carmel asked.

"*Ja*, beautiful Anna. She is my wife." Orm pressed his hands over his heart. "She took me as her husband when I thought no one ever would. I am… How would you say…" He spun his finger by his temple. "An acquired taste."

He certainly was that.

"Congratulations," Carmel said. "I am pleased for you both." She remembered the way Anna had looked at Orm, sought him out, found things to talk to him about. She wasn't that surprised about the news. Anna had clearly liked Orm…a lot.

"I am glad you have found the happiness I have," Ravn said. "And what is the news of King Haakon and our sister, Astrid?"

"Ah, there is much to tell."

"Go on," Carmel said, settling back and folding her arms. She was keen for news.

"Haakon is to be a father," Orm said, his eyes sparkling, "and judging by the size of Kenna's belly, I would wager it's twin boys."

"Really?" Ravn strode to the pit house. "We should celebrate," he called. "I will get the mead."

"Wait, brother." Orm held up his hand. "My wife wishes to get to Drangar after a long journey and I do not wish for her to swim to shore." He gestured at the longboat bobbing on the water. "We will celebrate in Drangar, together, when you return from this…this sea air vacation."

Ravn paused and nodded. "Very well. But before you go, tell me, how is Astrid?"

"Ah, Astrid." Orm rubbed his hands together. "She is as wild as ever and her man does nothing to tame her. Not one thing to rein her in, fasten her down, or hog-tie her."

"Her man. You mean Hamish?" Ravn asked.

"*Ja*, he's her man. He'll only ever be her man, for she refuses to marry him."

"Has he asked?" Ravn shrugged.

Orm laughed. "He knows her well enough to know that would get him no pussy for a week at least."

Carmel thought back to how Astrid had intimidated her. She had a fiery flash in her eyes that matched her hair and seemed beyond confident in her abilities, beliefs, and decisions.

"I miss her," Ravn said suddenly.

"You do?" Carmel asked.

"Really?" Orm raised his eyebrows.

"*Ja*, when you were sick, Carmel, I wished she were with me." Ravn stroked his hand over Carmel's hair. "I wished for her calmness and wisdom."

"You were sick?" Orm asked.

"My throat burned and the sweats took over my body."

Orm peered at her. "You are white, like the first snow."

"Which is why she must rest here." Ravn moved to Orm and in a sudden flurry, embraced him. "I'm glad that you are returned to your homeland. Father would have been too—"

"Huh, I'm not so sure about that."

"He would be glad to see you happy and married. Now go and I will look forward to our time together in Drangar. But until then, go to our people and let them be joyous about your marriage. They will be curious about Anna, as they were about Carmel."

"Aye, tell her not to be afraid, they are friendly," Carmel said. "Welcoming."

"I thank you, Your Grace, and I will pass that on. She has been troubled with not fitting in." He bowed low to her, almost mockingly.

"She has lots to learn," Carmel said calmly. "And I will be glad of her friendship when I return home."

"You have learned a lot. You speak our tongue now." Orm nodded approvingly. "It is a good sign that you will rule well."

Before Carmel could answer, he jumped into the air, clapped, then landed, puffing up dirt and sand with his boots. "I must love you and leave you, King and Queen. Until we meet again, be well and safe and fuck gloriously."

"But why did you come back?" Ravn called to his back. "Will you stay?"

Orm was running down the beach. "Over mead. I will tell you all over a horn or ten of mead." Orm held his hand in the air and ran into the waves. Within seconds, he'd disappeared under the water and then was striking out toward the longboat.

"That was unexpected." Ravn removed his weapons and then placed his hands on his hips.

"Very." Carmel stood and went to him.

"Why do you think he made the journey?" He took her into his arms.

"You all have the sea in your veins. Your blood is laced with saltwater. 'Haps the ocean called to him. 'Haps his home called to him. Maybe he wanted to show the world his pretty bride." She paused. "It could be he wanted to see you."

"He's never liked me." Ravn tutted. "Why would he want to see me?"

"That wasn't what I just witnessed." She stroked his hair, tucking it behind his ears. "He just jumped off a boat to swim and see you. That isn't something you do for someone you don't like."

Ravn appeared thoughtful. "You're very wise, you know that?"

"And you are caring and bossy, clever, and yet sometimes slow. And also, you are a fine warrior and seafarer and…"

"Keep going." He grinned. "This is fun."

"And glorious at fucking."

His eyes widened a moment, then he laughed. "You repeat my brother's crude words. That is not like you."

"Are you complaining?"

"No." He sat on the chair and smiled up at her. "I think I like it."

"Then you will like this." She straddled him and reached for his belt buckle. Within a few seconds, it was undone and hanging aside.

"Carmel," he said as he watched her undo the tie on his pants. "You are still…"

"I am not sick. I am almost well, and I think you are the last dose of medicine I need."

"Then I am at your service." He ran his wide palms up her thighs, gathering her tunic and exposing her bare pussy. He swallowed and licked his lips as he looked at her patch of hair.

"Is the longboat gone?" she asked, slipping her hand into his pants and gripping his cock.

He grunted as she wrapped her hand around his growing hardness. "It is…" He looked over her shoulder. "Going out of view very soon, around the headland."

"That is good, because I'm going to sit on your cock."

He laughed, a shocked huff of sound. "Your illness has left you with a wicked mouth."

She smiled and freed his cock entirely. "It's liberating."

"It's the way Vikings speak."

"Which you wanted from me."

"*Ja.*" He closed his eyes and breathed deeply. "Fuck, it feels good when you touch me like that."

She worked his length in several steady, firm strokes. It rose to full hardness and as always, it amazed her how quickly her husband could go from flaccid to steeliness in seconds. His cock was always ready for fucking, always willing to spill seed into her.

"The longboat has gone," he said, opening his eyes. "We are alone."

"Good." She lifted up and placed one hand on his shoulder for balance. "You should see if I am wet for you."

His eyes sparkled. "I should?"

"Aye, finger me." Carmel knew she'd just learned something else about her husband. He liked whispered dirty words. She'd remember that for the future.

He slipped his touch to her pussy, which was hovering over his cock. With his eye contact steady, he fingered through her folds, just brushing her nub.

She caught her breath, her breasts hitching.

"*Ja*," he murmured. "You are wet like a dewy morn." He explored further, to her entrance, and pushed in.

She groaned, loving his invasion. It was a prelude to more. Much more.

"Always wet and willing," he murmured, pushing in deeper. "My beautiful wife."

"Oh, aye, I am and…oh…Ravn."

She rocked her hips and the heel of his hand caught on her nub. Her fingers tightened on his shoulder and she closed her eyes. The first spark was already there and she stoked it by rolling her hips, a small dance that felt oh-so-good, especially when he added another finger.

"My love," he murmured. "I am yours."

"As I am yours."

She opened her eyes and looked at his rapt expression. "I want your cock."

"My cock wants you." He withdrew and circled her waist, keeping her tunic bunched up in his hands.

She looked down at his thick, needy cock and positioned herself over it, her pussy kissing the tip.

"Sit," he said, his voice tight. "Sit on me."

Carmel didn't need asking twice and she lowered onto him,

taking his cockhead into her body and then pausing to adjust to the delicious stretch of his width.

"Mmm," he moaned, not thrusting upward, but letting her have control. "Keep going."

"Tell me how much you need it."

"More than the moon needs the stars, more than a sail need wind… Oh, fuck, Carmel, I need you." His grip on her waist increased and he pulled her down onto his cock.

She forced her tight muscles to relax and took his length. The sensation was so dense and thick and filled her so absolutely. Her ass landed on his thighs and she curled her fingers into his flesh. "Oh…that is so…"

"In the name of the gods, I'm so deep inside you," he said, a rise of color growing on his cheeks. "This feels amazing."

"You glad…you made…this chair?"

"Hell yeah."

She let her head fall back and tipped her face to the sky. He caught her crown in his palm and leaned forward to lick her throat.

She moaned and moved her hips forward and backward. The grinding motion caught her nub and she trembled with the need for more.

Ravn obviously enjoyed it too because he encouraged her, with his hands on her waist, to keep up the rocking motion.

She worked herself on him, grinding and crushing as she gasped and shook. Her toes pointed and her nipples ached. The pressure in her pussy was growing, becoming a boiling cauldron of need that would overspill.

"Don't…stop," he said, cupping her right breast. "Carmel."

"Oh… Oh… I'm going to…" The sensation was so sweet, her body well and truly alive again. "It's here…Ravn."

She opened her eyes and stared into his face as the moment of ecstasy reached a crescendo and then released. It was wild and feral. It was intense and breath-stealing.

"Ah, fuck!" he cried as he blasted into her, his body as hard as

the rocks around them and his cock throbbing inside her. "Fuck
ja…"

She clasped his face and kept staring into his eyes. Her pussy
pulsed with pleasure as white-hot bliss raced around her body.
Never had she felt so connected with another person. She could
see into his soul. The goodness of him was there. He was the
most amazing man she could have ever wish to meet.

"I love you so very much," she gasped. "I always will."

"As I love you." He was breathing fast, his nostrils flared, and
a few dots of sweat sat on his brow.

"Nothing will ever part us."

"Nothing. I swear on Thor's hammer, nothing will part us."
He kissed her, holding her close with his arms wound around her
body. The breeze lifted her hair and a gull called overhead.

Carmel had lost her father, been taken prisoner, traveled to
another land, and survived the throat sweats, and thank goodness
all that had happened, because it meant God had placed her right
where she belonged.

Here. With her Viking husband. King and Queen.

And happier than she'd ever imagined possible.

Epilogue

Meanwhile, at Castle Athol

QUEEN ELSPETH THE Pious of the Westlands, Lothlend perched upon her throne. Her son, Seamus, was on her husband's throne, and at her side. He sat with his small, pointed chin tipped and his fingers curled over the ornate wooden arms. His booted feet dangled. He was still so young, only eleven, and wouldn't be able to truly rule until his feet touched the floor of the royal Athol throne.

If she were called away, she'd have to appoint a regent. And right now, that looked like a distinct possibility. There had been no word from her husband, or her daughter, and that gave her a dark, gnawing sensation in the very depths of her soul.

Something was wrong.

The battle in the east hadn't gone their way.

She just knew it. Somehow.

"Enough. Go!" She waved her hand, the harpist who had been entertaining them suddenly annoying, grating in her ears, rattling around her brain.

"Your Grace. Your Grace." A servant ran into the room, his steps heavy on the stone floor. "There is a messenger, just arrived." He pointed at the lead-paned window that led to the courtyard. The sun shone through it, marking the floor in small, golden squares.

She stood, her long, scarlet gown falling around her ankles. She clutched her rosary. "He has come from the east?"

"Aye, Your Grace, I'd wager so."

"Mother?" Her son slipped his hand into hers. "What is happening?"

"Perhaps we will finally get news." Her knees weakened, and a hollow pit opened up in her stomach. Were the words she was dreading about to be delivered?

Lord have mercy on us.

Please let it not be so.

A maid came to her side holding a goblet of sweet rosehip wine.

She took it, drank deep, then handed it back.

"Your Grace." A puce-faced soldier rushed into the room and came to a stop at the end of the long, emerald-green rug. His boots were caked in mud and a cut slashed over his left cheek. His bloodstained sword hung from a belt at his side. "I have news."

"So spit it out." She frowned at him.

"It is news of the battle at Tillicoulty." He was breathing heavily, his hands balled into fists. "There was much loss…a terrible defeat."

"And?" She squeezed her son's hand. "What of the king? What of my daughter, Princess Carmel?"

"The king is dead." The soldier crossed himself. "Dear God have mercy upon his soul."

"Oh, dear Lord." She sat heavily and Seamus crawled up onto her lap, even though he was really too big to sit there, and pressed close. She drew him in to a hug. "You are sure?"

"Aye, I saw his head upon a… I mean, I saw him killed with my own eyes." He closed his eyes, tightly, as though wishing he hadn't witnessed the macabre event.

"And…" Elspeth swallowed, it was as though thorns were grating on her throat. "Carmel, my beautiful princess daughter. What of her?"

"Captive, Your Grace. She was taken by the heathens who have overrun Tillicoulty and claimed it for themselves. They have taken her."

"'Taken'? 'Captive'?" Elspeth stood once more, Seamus landing at her side and pushing into her gowns so that his face was half-covered. "And you did not recover her?"

"No, Your Grace."

"Why, in the name of the good Lord, didn't you?" She should have him hanged for this, swinging from the scaffold by nightfall.

"I beg your forgiveness. But there are too many of them, and they fight as though the devil himself is at their side. Monsters, that's what they are. The women too. All monsters with crazed eyes and skills that could only have been honed in hell."

She shuddered at the thought of such monstrous men, such violence, such evil that had landed on their peaceful shores.

"Where is Carmel?" Seamus asked, tugging on her skirt. "I want to see her."

"She is in a dangerous place," Elspeth said before drawing in a deep breath. She calmed herself. She had to think straight. If she didn't, who would? "A wicked and dangerous place far from here, Seamus."

"It has been a four-day ride at full pace, Your Grace," the soldier said. "With rough terrain and many rivers to navigate."

"I appreciate your swift delivery of this news, awful as it is." She nodded at a servant. "Give him three gold coins."

"Thank you." The soldier bobbed his head, clearly relieved that he wasn't going to be punished for being the bearer of bad news.

"Mother," Seamus said. "What is to be done?"

She looked down at his sweet, childish face, yet to show the features he'd have as a man. His big, green eyes stared up at her as though she, and she alone, could fix every problem in the world. All he had to do was ask.

It was the same way her precious Carmel had looked at her once upon a time.

She pulled in a deep breath and something in her heart squeezed a new force of determination into her. It was hot and vibrant and undefeatable. There was only one thing she could do and that was go get her daughter back herself.

An army? Trade? Diplomacy? She wasn't sure, but what she did know was that she had only herself to rely on.

Because right now, her sweet, virginal daughter was being held by heathens who had no qualms about rape and pillage and murder and had no respect for Jesus Christ or the Lord God.

She, Queen Elspeth the Pius, was the only person in the world who could fix this god-awful situation, and she would damn well do that.

Starting now.

About the Author

Based in the UK, Lily Harlem is an award-winning, *USA Today* bestselling author of sexy romance. She's a complete floozy when it comes to genres and pairings, writing saucy historical, heterosexual kink, gay paranormal, and everything in between. She's also very partial to a happily ever after.

If you're a Kindle Unlimited subscriber, you can read many of her books for free, including several complete series, and if you love sporty romances, get the first novel in her popular HOT ICE series when you sign up for her newsletter.

One thing you can be sure of, whatever book you pick up by Ms. Harlem, is it will be wildly romantic and deliciously sexy. Enjoy!

Website: www.lilyharlem.com
Amazon Author Page: author.to/LilyHarlem
Lily's Reader Group: facebook.com/groups/188731774881774

Find your next book boyfriend…
Male/Female
Male/Male
Historical Romance
Paranormal
Menage a Trois
Reverse Harem
Audio Books

For more deliciously steamy historical romance, including a plethora of stern Highlanders, dashing dukes, and kinky Vikings, visit Lily's website.

9 781969 349096